FLYING LESSONS
& other stories

Edited by Ellen Oh
With Foreword by Christopher Myers

A Yearling Book

This book is dedicated to the memory of
Walter Dean Myers, who said, "There is work to be done."
So our work continues. —Ellen Oh

"Welcome to the Neighborhood" copyright © 2018 by Christopher Myers.
"Editor's Note" copyright © 2017 by Ellen Oh.
"How to Transform an Everyday, Ordinary Hoop Court
into a Place of Higher Learning and You at the Podium" copyright © 2017
by Matt de la Peña. "The Difficult Path" copyright © 2017 by Grace Lin.
"Sol Painting, Inc." copyright © 2017 by Meg Medina. "Secret Samantha"
copyright © 2017 by Tim Federle. "The Beans and Rice Chronicles of Isaiah
Dunn" copyright © 2017 by Kelly J. Baptist. "Choctaw Bigfoot, Midnight in the
Mountains" copyright © 2017 by Tim Tingle. "Main Street" copyright © 2017
by Jacqueline Woodson. "Flying Lessons" copyright © 2017 by Soman Chainani.
"Seventy-Six Dollars and Forty-Nine Cents" copyright © 2017 by
Kwame Alexander. "Sometimes a Dream Needs a Push" copyright © 2017
by Walter Dean Myers, first appeared in *Boys' Life* in 2007.

All rights reserved. Published in the United States by Yearling, an imprint of Random House Children's Books, a division of Penguin Random House LLC, New York. Originally published in hardcover by Crown Books for Young Readers, an imprint of Random House Children's Books, New York, in 2017.

Yearling and the jumping horse design
are registered trademarks of Penguin Random House LLC.

Visit us on the Web! rhcbooks.com

Educators and librarians, for a variety of teaching tools,
visit us at RHTeachersLibrarians.com

Library of Congress Cataloging-in-Publication Data is available upon request.
ISBN 978-1-101-93459-3 (trade) — ISBN 978-1-101-93460-9 (lib. bdg.) —
ISBN 978-1-101-93461-6 (ebook) — ISBN 978-1-101-93462-3 (trade pbk.)

Printed in the United States of America
10 9 8 7 6 5 4 3 2 1
First Yearling Edition 2018

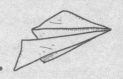

Contents

Welcome to the Neighborhood
CHRISTOPHER MYERS

My father, Walter, loved to cook. He spent hours in the kitchen, tending pots and sauces, careful as a deejay selecting music at a house party. When I would invite a friend over, he'd ask what the friend couldn't eat before he'd ask their name. He'd make a menu, Google a few things, wander through Chinatown or Curry Hill or Little Italy gathering ingredients, and arrive home, proceeding to make more food than any of us could eat. He taught me what it meant to have guests; you had to take care of them.

Pop practiced a kind of hospitality, the importance of making people feel welcome. It's a trait I'm happy to have learned to recognize in others as I've traveled the world.

In Kibera, a massive slum in Nairobi, I entered a makeshift home of found corrugated metal sheets woven together, with daylight and wind creeping in between the crevices. A woman offered me a bottle of cola and a chair, moments before I realized it was the only piece of furniture in the home. In Jogjakarta, at a computer-repair shop, there was a cup of tea; in Cairo, a woman asked if I would like some of what she was eating.

Poppa learned this hospitality thing, growing up in a home in which there was never much, but always enough to share with your neighbors and friends if they needed it. I've found he practiced that same sort of hospitality in his writing, extending an invitation to the reader that said, "No matter what harrowing or amazing tale you will experience in this book, know you are welcome here. Let me share with you what I have, and we will enjoy the sharing."

Books are homes, have been homes, will continue to be homes. They are places we can go when we have no other place. For my father in Harlem, caught between seemingly unreachable dreams and the realities of race and poverty in the United States, books provided possibility, comfort, and challenge. He knew it is important that the readers feel welcome, feel that sense of hospitality. It is our job as writers to invite you in.

Poppa found that invitation in so many kinds of books and stories, from Louisa May Alcott and James Joyce to

Gabriela Mistral and Juan Ramón Jiménez. But there were also moments when he didn't know if he was welcome. And for those of us who have ever been in a place where we weren't wanted, there are few feelings that are worse. It wasn't until he encountered the work of James Baldwin that my father read a book that felt like it had been written *for* him. One measure of Baldwin's art is the extent of invitation readers, even today, feel in his work. The same could be said for Poppa's books.

Imagine then this book you are holding, *Flying Lessons*, as series of homes, of stories, a neighborhood of story-houses, and you are invited into them all. Please make yourself comfortable. Each story, each kind of storytelling, is different, but you are welcome in all of them. Join Grace Lin on a creaking ship, and listen to the poetry of Li Po with her. (Incidentally, Pop loved Li Po's poems, too.) Matt de la Peña's basketball court is next. It is more than a court, undoubtedly, but whatever it is, you got next game. Jackie Woodson invites you to New Hampshire, to a place where none of us perhaps feel at home, but then again perhaps the feeling of isolation and the recognition of that feeling is an invitation, too.

Here is a collection of homes, of stories, of hosts who have traveled through their city tending to their words as carefully as a deejay selecting music at a house party. You are our guest. Welcome to the neighborhood.

Editor's Note

Dear Reader,

When I was little, I found an abandoned kitten on the street. It was mangy, flea-ridden, and mean, but so cute. I loved it. We lived in an apartment building that had a NO PETS ALLOWED sign in the lobby. But I didn't care. I'd always wanted a pet. I mean, I had a baby sister, but she wasn't as fun as a kitten. I was determined to take it home, even though I knew my parents would be mad because it was against the rules. So I scooped George up—yeah, I had already decided to name him George—tucked him close to my chest, and headed for home.

By the time I walked the five blocks to my building, I was a wreck. I looked like a monster. Not only did George manage to scratch up my entire face and chest, but he also taught me that I was terribly allergic to cats. My eyes swelled into leaky water balloons, and I was covered in huge welts that looked like radioactive leeches had attached themselves all over my body. My parents totally freaked out.

When my dad took George away from me, I whisper-yelled through my swollen throat, "That's my cat!" As I reached for my pet, he hissed at me and scratched me one last time in good-bye.

Turns out George wasn't alone. All cats hate me. Which is why I now own a dog. But I'll never forget George. He's the story my parents loved to bring up at every family re-union. About how I saved a poor orphaned kitten that tried to kill me.

But we all have stories like that, right? They might be milk-snorting-out-of-your-nose funny ones, or listen-to-how-cool-and-awesome-we-are ones, or come-close-so-we-can-whisper-in-your-ear juicy ones. They might be old favorites or stories about new experiences. But no matter what, our stories are unique, just like we are. And that is what this book is all about—ten diverse stories from ten great authors. For all of us.

Ellen Oh

How to Transform an Everyday, Ordinary Hoop Court into a Place of Higher Learning and You at the Podium

MATT DE LA PEÑA

It's finally summer.

Go ahead, take a deep breath. You're free.

All year long your moms has been on you like glue about algebra worksheets and science fair projects and the knee-high stack of books Mrs. Baker assigned for English class. And you did what you had to do. Two As and four Bs.

Truth is, you're actually pretty smart.

School comes easy.

You told Baker in that end-of-the-year five-page paper what was up with Esperanza's dreams and the symbolism of the Mango Street house, and you pulled down a 96 percent—second-highest grade in the class. But even as you typed out that essay, you had an indoor-outdoor in your lap. Between sentences you daydreamed finger rolls over outstretched hands.

See, here's what all the hard-core homework pushers don't get.

For people like you, ball is more than just ball.

It's a way out.

A path to those tree-lined lives they always show on TV.

You've crunched the numbers and read the tea leaves. Fact is, you'll *never* hit the books as hard as Boy Genius Jeremiah Villa. Sylvia Diaz, either. Even your boy Francisco, from down the hall. There are folks in this world who live to mark up a fat World History textbook with an arsenal of colored highlighters.

You're not one of them.

You spend too much time on back-alley ball-handling drills to compete.

Nah, the game of basketball is *your* best chance.

The Fate of Your Hoop Development

For the past three years you've spent every free minute balling at an outdoor court down the street from your building. After school. After games. Weekends. You name it.

Most nights you're still out there putting up shots, alone, when the sun falls behind the ocean and the automatic park lights come flickering on, spilling that strange yellow halflight across the cracked concrete.

Ball is like anything else.

2

Put in enough hours, your game's gonna blast off.

Your jumper's now pure out to twenty-five feet, give or take. You've developed a little floater in the lane that leaves slow-footed big men flailing. But it's your handle that sets you apart. Your quicks. The way you can get into the paint at will and finish with either hand.

This past season you scored more points than any other eighth grader in the county.

You were second in assists.

So what.

It ain't good enough, and you know it.

Not if you want to be even *more* dominant next year, in high school.

That's why your ears perk up when you overhear a couple newcomers talking about Muni Gym in Balboa Park. When you overhear the dude with love handles sitting on the stairs say to his boy, "It's the best run in the entire city, B. I put that on everything."

"You ranked 'em out?" the other guy asks.

"Nah, I used to ball there all the time before I tweaked my back. If you can hang with them big boys at Muni . . . shoot, you can hang with just about anybody."

Shelf the extra jumpers that night.

Proceed instead to the local library and look up Muni Gym online. Type the address into Google Earth and you'll discover it's right next to the Air and Space Museum your

3

moms took you and your sis to back in the day. And the Air and Space Museum, if your calculations are correct, isn't but five miles from your pop's job at the factory.

Wander into your cramped living room after dinner that night. Work up the guts to describe for your old man the importance of competing against the best. You've outgrown your local run. It's time to put a foot in the deep end. So what if he doesn't even know the rules of the game, if all he does is sit there silently inside the TV, working a toothpick in his teeth.

"So, what do you think, Pop?"

"About what?"

"Would it be cool if I went with you to work every morning? So I could play some ball down there?"

He'll look at you suspiciously, then turn back to his cop show and his toothpick.

You'll take this as a no and assume the fate of the most important summer of your hoop development now rests in the hands of the county bus system.

But you'll be wrong.

A few minutes later he'll mumble, "Better have your skinny butt out by the car by five, I'll tell you that. Or else I'm leaving without you."

He won't even look up when he tells you this.

Doesn't matter.

Your heart will race with excitement.

You'll tear into the room you share with your sis and lay your hoop gear out on the chair by your bed like some kind of giddy schoolgirl—which is pretty much how you'll feel.

There's Only Today

Know that when your alarm starts blaring at four-thirty the next morning, you're going to have no idea where you are or what's happening. It'll still be dark outside. Your sis will be snoring. When reality finally settles in, the lazy part of your brain will try and sweet-talk you back to sleep: *Maybe we could, you know, skip the Muni trip today . . . go ball at the park instead. . . . There's always tomorrow.*

Reach into your own skull and smack this part of your brain upside the head.

If you let it, this part of your brain will hold you back from every dream you will ever have. Trust me.

Crawl out of bed, reminding yourself that your old man gets up like this every single day for work. Rain or shine. In sickness and in health.

Your uncles, too.

Respect them for this.

Strive to be like them.

During the entire thirty-minute drive south, your old man will say two sentences to you, max. Don't take it personally. Answer his question about the gym location and how you

5

heard about it. Buckle your seat belt when he gives you one of his patented dirty looks. Before you even hit the freeway on-ramp you'll be done talking, but that's okay. Shift your focus to other details of the drive. The radio news show he turns on. The smell of his steaming-hot black coffee. The scattered cars along the dark freeway, and the subtle tick of his turn signal whenever he changes lanes. By the end of summer, these seemingly insignificant details will be ingrained in your brain.

When he parks along the street near his factory, it'll still be a full three hours before Muni Gym opens. "Better have your skinny butt back here by quarter to four," he'll say, snatching his lunch pail out of the backseat. "It's a long walk home, I'll tell you that."

After he disappears around the bend, turn your attention to the ancient Volkswagen Bug. You'll wonder how the heck you're supposed to sleep inside such a tiny car, but after a little trial and error you'll find a way. It will involve folding your six-foot-one frame into a kind of human pretzel. Half of you will be in the backseat, while the other half is curled up into the front passenger seat, your bag strategically lodged into the center console to keep the hand brake from digging into your ribs.

By day three, this next-level yoga position will feel perfectly natural.

But let's get something straight from the jump. This Muni

Gym summer isn't going to be some kind of continuous loop of "One Shining Moment." There'll be low points, too. On *and* off the court. Trust me.

A few weeks in, a meaty-faced cop will knock on the windshield with the butt of his nightstick. He'll look at you through aviator sunglasses, his right hand resting on a holstered handgun.

Try not to panic.

His suspicions will be based on two simple facts:

1. This is the first time during his rounds he's ever stumbled across a kid sleeping at a ninety-degree angle inside a VW Bug.
2. Your skin is brown.
2a. (His skin will be brown, too—maybe even *browner*—but don't spend too much time worrying yourself about this. There's a complex psychology behind this phenomenon, one you're not yet ready to wrap your head around.)

At the end of your respectful explanation, the cop will slowly remove his hand from his gun. He'll grab hold of your left elbow instead and steer you toward the front office of the factory. Your pop will be summoned, embarrassingly, over the loudspeaker. Two minutes later he'll emerge from the back looking wildly stressed. This is not because you've done anything wrong. It's because he has his own history with cops. Stuff that happened long before you were born. Stuff nobody ever talks about.

After the cop explains the situation, your pop will put on an uncomfortable smile and vouch for you. He'll say you're a good kid, that you're just down here to play some ball at a gym in Balboa Park. He'll shake hands with the cop enthusiastically, thanking him for his service and apologizing for any trouble you may have caused.

Soon as the cop leaves, though, your pops will transform back into himself. "Don't worry about that power-happy pendejo," he'll say, rubbing your shoulder. "You didn't do nothing wrong."

"I was just sleeping."

"Mexicans are allowed to sleep, too." He'll look you straight in the eyes, nodding. And in this moment, you'll feel closer to your old man than ever before.

Fortunately, that's the only morning you'll be woken up by a nightstick. Every other morning it'll be the alarm on your phone, and you'll be free to climb out of the Bug at your leisure. Stretch your stiff arms and legs. Breathe in the warm Hillcrest air and remove your rock from your bag. It's time to get a move on.

It won't take but three days to know all the shortcuts to Muni.

Dribble through the middle school playground where

summer camp kids play double Dutch and hopscotch and dodgeball. Dribble in and out of sleeping cars in the massive San Diego Zoo parking lot. Dribble through crowds of camera-toting tourists shuffling toward the front gates of the zoo. Dribble past the various hot dog stands, the ice cream truck with the two flat tires, the leather-faced man selling raspas who looks like your late abuelito. By the end of the summer these vendors will all recognize you and wave.

It will take a little more than an hour for you to arrive at the large, dilapidated building with two locked green doors. Butterflies will dance inside your chest. That first time and every time following. Even years from now. And that's how it *should* be.

Because you can sense it . . .

Here is where you will learn the world.

Sentenced to the Bleachers

While you wait for gym manager Jimmy to arrive by bicycle with his massive ring of rattling keys, listen to the grown men around you. To the uninitiated they are uneducated. They're poor. Black. Crass. Shifty. Steely-eyed. A reason to cross the street.

But over the course of the summer you will soak up everything around you. And you will hear the brilliance.

The poetry. The philosophy. The verbal dance of on-court banter. They will laugh harder and more often than anyone you've ever known. And you will laugh, too. Especially a few weeks into the summer, when they turn their wrath on you.

They'll begin by calling you Mexico (even though your Spanish is suspect at best). They will ask why you're inside a gym, and not crouched in a field somewhere, picking strawberries. Or kicking around a soccer ball. They will tell you you're too young to ball with them. Too skinny. Too light in the pocket. Too soft.

Come back in three years, they'll say.

Or maybe ten.

You will laugh your way through all of this, sensing that their digs are some warped version of acceptance.

A week in, a guy everyone calls Mr. Unleaded (because he's the night manager of a nearby gas station) will tear into you about your long, skinny, "no-muscle-having" arms, and without blinking you'll fire back a dig about the ghetto Superman tat sketched into his right forearm, and "Why would you knowingly walk into a gym full of Kryptonite?" Everyone loitering outside the gym that morning, waiting for Jimmy, will roar in laughter and stomp their feet and bump fists, and to your surprise it'll be Mr. Unleaded who laughs hardest of all.

But as much as you'll begin to blend in off the court, on the court it will be a completely different story.

That first day you won't get into a single game.

Not *one*.

You'll follow everyone inside the dark gym, set down your stuff in the bleachers like they do, hit the court with everyone for a handful of warm-up jumpers, but when it comes time to select squads, you'll find yourself on the outside looking in.

When you try to call next, they'll ignore you.

You'll ask the overweight knee-braced dude if you can run with *his* squad. He's still three games away, but you got all day. He'll nod and say in a deep smoker voice, "You down, young buck. I got you." But an hour later, when his team is finally set to take the court, he'll drop you for a balding big man.

At first this basketball blackballing will tear you up inside. You know you can hang. Your jumper is as pure as anyone's in the gym (except maybe this guy they call Dante, who never misses). Sure, these dudes are bigger and stronger and more aggressive, but at the very least you could be a dependable distributor. You know where to put a lob on the fast break so your big man can mash it down with a guttural growl.

You plead with the guys standing on the sidelines. "You gotta let me play, man. I can ball. I swear." But these outbursts of self-promotion will fall on deaf ears. All you'll do that first day is hoist a few jumpers between games, then retreat back to the bleachers to watch.

The next day it'll be the same thing.

The day after that.

Those first two weeks you'll participate in a grand total of one run—if you can even count the end-of-the-day, three-on-three debacle you spend guarding a homeless man wearing soleless Timberlands.

One afternoon it'll hit you especially hard on the long walk back to the car.

You'll keep quiet on the drive home, then retreat to an overturned bucket in the alley behind your building, where you'll have a serious heart-to-heart with yourself. Sure, it's the best pickup you've ever seen, but they don't even let you play. They're prejudiced against Mexicans. Or soon-to-be ninth graders. Or both. Why wake up before the crack of dawn, sleep folded up in a VW Bug, just to sit in the bleachers all day?

Nah, man, this won't work.

You're a baller, not a spectator.

At least at the court down the street you can work up a sweat.

On your way into your room that night, you'll break the news to your old man. "Just so you know, Pop, I'm not driving down with you anymore. Thanks for taking me all those times."

He'll look up from his beer with a frown. "What happened?"

You're a pretty tough kid. Nothing much gets to you. But for some reason his question will put a lump in your throat. "It's just . . . I don't even know why, but they won't let me play."

Secretly you'll be hoping for a little piece of fatherly advice here, but you won't get it. He'll chuckle instead and turn back to his beer.

You won't set your alarm that night. You'll sink into bed, excited by the thought of sleeping in. Relieved to be downshifting back into the old routine.

But something odd will happen.

The next morning your body will instinctively wake up at four-thirty. You'll sit up, rubbing your eyes, confused. Your hands will unconsciously reach into the dirty clothes for your hoop gear, and your feet, against executive orders, will carry you out to the car a few minutes before five.

When your old man sees you standing there, he'll chuckle again.

But he won't say anything.

Don't Just Sit There Like a Punk

It won't be until week four that you finally get into a meaningful game.

By this time you'll know most of the guys by nickname. And you'll know how they play. At some point your focus

13

will have shifted from wanting to play, to breaking down their various skill sets. There's one guy in particular you'll study.

Dante.

He's six four and thin. In his early thirties maybe. He's the only guy in the gym who's never said a word to you. He walks right by like you don't even exist. But he can seriously play. Not only does he knock down almost every jumper he takes, he hardly ever grazes the rim. He has this sweet little fadeaway in the post, and whenever someone tries to challenge him on the break, they get mashed on, posterized, and guys on the sidelines fall all over each other, laughing and stomping and pointing.

After burying one particular game winner from the wing, two guys draped all over him, he'll turn to you suddenly and bark, "Hey, kid, why you still coming here?"

You pause your dribble, stunned. "Who me?"

"Nobody thinks you're good enough to play here, comprende? Why don't you go on back to the barrio, esé."

Your whole body will freeze up from the shock of his words.

Everyone in the entire gym inching closer, waiting to see what happens next.

Dante strides over and points a finger in your face. "What, are you deaf, kid? I said leave!"

No words form in your brain.

No thoughts.

Dante spins to the rest of the guys. "Someone get this scrub out my face before I do something stupid."

A couple regulars will lead you toward the bleachers, but your legs aren't quite working yet. You're confused almost to the point of paralysis. Because what did you do wrong? Why does he hate you? Your heart thump-thump-thumping inside your chest. Doubt setting in. Maybe he's right. Maybe you really *are* a scrub. Maybe you *shouldn't* be allowed to show up like this every day, uninvited.

Maybe the whole summer has been one big mistake.

You grab your stuff off the bleachers and start toward the door, but for some unexplainable reason you stop. You turn around. You glare across the court at Dante, mumbling, "I just wanna play."

"What?" Dante shouts back. He picks up a ball and fires it at you, narrowly missing. "Speak up if you got something to say!"

"I wanna play," you repeat, louder this time.

"What?"

"I wanna play!"

A few of the guys start toward you again, wanting to get you out of the gym before you get hurt, but Dante puts a stop to that. "Get away from him! This is between me and the kid!"

The whole gym silent aside from your heartbeat.

Your short, nervous breaths measuring the time.

"Check it out," Dante suddenly announces. "The kid's got my spot this game." Then he turns back to you. "After you get smoked, you walk out them doors and never come back, you hear?"

You stand there studying him for a few extra beats, searching for his angle, trying to decide if it's some kind of trick, if you're still in danger. Before your ruling is in, though, you find yourself being shoved out onto the court.

"You got Dollar Bill," someone is telling you.

It takes a minute to realize what's happening.

They're letting you play.

And if you mess up, it's over.

As fast as your heart was beating when Dante got in your face, it slows back down once the ball is in play. Because this is the one place in the entire world where you're truly alive. Where your brain shuts off and every move is made on instinct.

It only takes two trips up and down before you shake off the cobwebs and slip into the flow. First time the ball gets swung to you out on the wing, you skip past your defender and spin into the lane for a little ten-foot bank shot off the glass.

A few guys on the sideline oohing and aahing.

A few plays later you bury an open twenty-footer, nothing but net, Dante style.

You rip Dollar Bill near half court and race down the floor for a little finger roll over the rim. And as you retreat back down for defense after that one, you can hear the gym erupting.

Now you're buried deep inside the folds of the game.

The outside world slinks off and hides, and all you know are the choreographed movements around you. The dance. The beautiful symphony of squeaking sneaks and grunts and the thud of body meeting body. Each man's heavy breath and his eyes like a portal to his mind.

You bury two more deep jumpers, followed by a game-winning scoop shot in the lane, which results in the other team's big man tripping over his own feet and falling on his face.

The guys on your squad mob you near midcourt.

"That's right, young buck," they say.

"That's how you let fools know," they say.

A few go on about how they've been meaning to pick you up all summer, they just never got a chance, blah, blah, blah.

But just as you're starting to feel yourself, Dante will be back in your grill. "What, you make a couple jumpers, and now you supposed to be somebody?"

"No, I just—"

"Get off my court, kid."

"But—"

He'll grab you by the arm and fling you toward the bleachers, barking to everyone else, "Yo, I got my spot back! Check ball!"

You'll consider putting up a fight here, but don't.

Trust me.

What matters is you'll have proven you can play. What matters is every head who saw what you just did will see you differently now. As proof, not thirty seconds later a guy who goes by the name of Slim will wander over and say, "Yo, young buck, I got next. Wanna run with me?"

"For sure."

Rob will overhear this exchange and bark, "Yo, Slim, I thought you already had five. Who you dropping?"

"You."

"Me?"

"You just seen this boy's skills, right? I gotta get me a point guard."

"But you said I was down, Slim. Don't play your boy like that. . . ."

In the middle of this debate, a stray jumper will roll out of bounds toward you, and Dante will give chase. He'll grab the rock and kneel down, not five feet from you, to tie his shoe. "Hey, kid," he'll say in a quiet voice.

"Yeah?"

He'll look up at you, mid–double knot. "You wanna get in games, you don't just sit there like a punk, right? You stand up and challenge the baddest dude in the gym. Someone like me. Then you do your thing. Understand?"

His intense eyes will be like knives inside your chest. "Yes, sir."

He'll stand up and nod, then jog back onto the court, shouting, "Yo, check ball! Let's go!"

You'll think this is the beginning of some meaningful mentorship, but it won't be. In fact, Dante won't say another word to you the rest of the summer. Not even when you ask him a direct question. But over time you'll begin to see the power of his silence. And surprisingly, it will remind you of your old man's silence.

A few months into your ninth-grade season, you'll actually spot Dante in the stands at one of your games. He'll be alone, eating popcorn, watching. You'll be the starting point guard on the varsity squad—which is pretty legit for a freshman. And you'll be having your best game of the young season. You'll wave as you jog past him at halftime, but he won't wave back. He'll continue eating his popcorn. After the game you'll climb the packed bleachers looking for him, but he'll already be gone.

Your old man will be there, though.

And on the drive back to your apartment that night you'll realize something important. Your old man is always there. And he always has been. And so what if he doesn't say anything about how many points you just scored. How many assists. So what if he turns on his radio news show instead of breaking down the big win.

Maybe words aren't what's important.

Maybe words would just steal away your freedom to think for yourself.

What You Did This Summer

Your first class, on your first day of ninth grade, will be English with Mr. Howe.

Shuffle into the room with everyone else. Locate the desk with your name tag and take a seat. After Mr. Howe goes around the room, having everyone introduce themselves, he'll ask the class to pull out a sheet of paper. And he'll give you the first of the seventeen thousand writing prompts he'll assign over the course of the semester.

"This one's easy," he'll say. "All I want you to do is describe one thing you did this summer. And one thing you learned. You have fifteen minutes. Go!"

You'll moan and groan with everyone else, but once you start writing, the summer will come pouring out. You'll write about sleeping in the VW Bug and the cop knocking on the window and all the vendors you passed on the long walk and the way the old gym walls actually creaked on especially hot days and how the second half of the summer you got in all the games and the guys started calling you

Mexican Buckets and fighting over who had to guard you. But the time you spent on the actual court, you'll realize, was nowhere near as important as the time you spent in the bleachers. And you'll devote all your remaining time to describing one seemingly insignificant moment.

During your last week at the gym, Slim offered to buy you a hot dog and Coke for lunch. He claimed he was tired of watching you scoop handfuls of generic granola into your mouth every day. "You a growing boy, man. You need a balanced diet. Now let's go get you a hot dog and a Coke."

"No, thanks," you told him.

He looked at you surprised. "You sure? My treat."

"Nah, I'm good," you said. "But thanks."

"All right," he said, shrugging. "I guess you must really like that granola." And then he walked away.

Truth was, you turned him down that day because you knew he didn't have any money. He'd lost his security guard job at the start of summer. His shoes were falling apart and you heard he'd been evicted from his apartment.

Saying no, you thought, was the right thing to do.

But on the car ride home that afternoon, your pop shook his head in disappointment. He turned down his news show for the first time all summer. "When a man with nothing offers to give you something," he said, "you take it."

"You do?"

"Always."

"Why?"

He glanced at you as he merged onto the freeway. "You just do, all right?"

At the time it didn't make much sense. You saved Slim money. But as you write, you'll begin to see it differently. And you'll end the assignment by saying, "What I learned is that when a man who stays mostly quiet offers advice, you take it.

"You just do, all right?

"Trust me."

The Difficult Path

GRACE LIN

When I was sold to the Li family, my mother let Mrs. Li take me only after she'd promised that I would be taught to read. "Her mother had fourteen other children starving and clinging to her, yet she was still insisting that I promise." Mrs. Li sniffed and began a high-pitched imitation. " 'Promise me that when she's six, you'll have her taught to read! On your ancestors' grave! Promise!' "

"You didn't have to agree," Aunty Wang replied peevishly. This was a story she had already heard many times.

"A girl! Learn to read! What a waste!" Mrs. Li continued, her annoyance at the past greater than Aunty Wang's with the present. "Just because the mother had been a scholar's daughter!"

"Then you shouldn't have lied," Aunty Wang said,

rolling her eyes. She helped herself to some honeyed lychees I held.

"I thought she would never know!" Mrs. Li said. "I just said yes so that I could take the baby and go."

I made a soft coughing noise and placed the tray on the table.

"Mrs. Li," I said as I bowed low, "Teacher is here."

She snorted with irritation and waved her arm, her voluminous silk sleeve flapping like a flag of surrender. "Go," she dismissed me.

I hid my smile and tried to walk humbly, as all the browbeaten servants were supposed to do. Unlike Aunty Wang, however, I was not tired of Mrs. Li's complaining story. I had no memory of my mother, but hearing how she had dared to make demands of the formidable Mrs. Li on my behalf always made me feel a sense of pride. Despite my mother's poor circumstances, she must have been spirited.

And perhaps it was my mother's spirit that forced Mrs. Li to keep her promise. For on the day I turned six, a new tutor came to the House of Li. As I cringed during my daily duty of emptying the chamber pots, I saw the top of his black scholar's hat glide slowly past the family shrine into the schoolroom. He had come for Mrs. Li's repulsive only son, FuDing, of course. The learned scholar was yet another tutor hired in hopes that FuDing could be taught something. The last two teachers had departed in disgrace as well as anger. For, because FuDing remained unable to read a single poem, Mrs. Li had also refused the tutors' pay.

My birthday and a new tutor's entry should have been of small consequence to the House of Li, except it was also on that day that the incense of the ancestral shrine refused to light. Master Li tried again and again, but no matter how large a flame he held, the incense would not burn. In desperation, Master Li turned to the new tutor for answers.

"It is apparent," the scholar said, "that you or someone in your household has shamed your ancestors. Perhaps someone has stolen something or has broken a promise."

"Of course." Master Li nodded with respect. Then he snapped at Mrs. Li. "Wife! We have angered our ancestors! What have you done?"

The House of Li roared into a typhoon as all, from the head cook to the lowliest servant (me), were questioned. When it was discovered that it was my sixth birthday, Mrs. Li remembered her promise to my mother, then paled and swayed like a blanched stalk of bamboo.

"It couldn't be . . . ," she said in horror.

But it could be and probably was, the new tutor said, and immediately quoted his price for two students. Mrs. Li, still aghast at the revelation and fending off insults from her husband, did not even haggle over the price. (She did try later, claiming that as a girl I should be cheaper, but he responded that because I was a girl he should be paid more, as he was making an exception, so the matter was dropped.) And I began my education.

That was over six years ago. It was also over six years ago that I saw my Teacher walk in with a new pair of shoes. Those shoes glided on the smooth stone floor, only hesitating as he paused in front of the shrine. With a sharp glance around, he quickly changed the incense—insuring my lessons and his larger salary.

"You are late, Lingsi!" Teacher said, but without anger. He knew Mrs. Li was always the reason for my tardiness.

"Lingsi is late!" FuDing sneered. I tried to consider FuDing with kindness, for it was his inability to read little more than his name that had granted me so many years of lessons. But it was difficult. His body had, over the years, grown into a man's, but he was still the same lazy, spoiled brat he had been as a boy. If anything, the years had made him even more horrible, for now he had a vicious streak that delighted in cruelty. I couldn't help shivering when I saw that he was pulling the legs off crickets again.

"Today's poem," Teacher said, ignoring FuDing, "is 'The Difficult Path' by Li Po."

I knelt at the table and began to read.

> *"I will ride the winds and*
> *Surmount endless waves.*
> *Setting sail on the vast ocean,*

I will one day reach
The distant shores."

"The ocean," I murmured. I had been outside the walled estate of the House of Li only a handful of times. However, one time Shuwan, the head cook, and I had been sent to town to buy pepper, and I had caught a glimpse of the sea. But only a glimpse, for when I tried to see more, I was yanked away. Shuwan had a terror of pirates and was convinced that just looking at the sea could make them appear.

"Li Po writes of endless hardships," Teacher said, "but you also feel his valiant spirit. I hope this is something you remember, Lingsi."

I looked up at him, the question in my eyes, since I dared not ask with my voice.

"Today is our last lesson," Teacher said. "Mrs. Li has informed me that FuDing will soon be of marrying age and his time must now be spent in . . . other ways."

We both glanced at FuDing, who was creating a pile of dead insects, and then quickly looked away. My eyes filled with tears. I had known that these lessons would not continue forever, but now that they were ending, I felt I could not bear it.

"You have learned much, Lingsi," Teacher said to me kindly. "You are a very smart and clever pupil. If you had been a boy, I have no doubt you would have won honors at the Imperial Examination."

I tried to smile but could only bow my head. I felt Teacher's hand gently rest upon it.

"Mencius, the Second Sage, said that there are three joys in this world," he said. "Health, a clear conscience, and teaching those who are worthy. Teaching you has been a joy, Lingsi."

My tears continued to drop long after our last lesson, long after Teacher had left the House of Li and I had swept up FuDing's collection of insects. They even continued as I scrubbed the pots in the kitchen, much to the annoyance of the other servants.

"Stop your crying," Bisi snapped, carrying over dirty bowls for me to wash. "We've got enough to do without listening to your sniffling."

"Look at me," Shuwan said. "I have to prepare lunch boxes for the entire household, and am I wailing? And Haobo and Mugang and all the men have to prepare the sedan chairs and get ready to carry fat FuDing for hours tomorrow, and they aren't crying, either. So your sniveling is not welcome!"

I gulped and rubbed my face with my sleeve. "Why are we getting lunch boxes and sedan chairs ready?" I asked. "Where is the family going?"

"Where are we all going, you mean," Bisi said. "They're taking all of us this time—even you."

"Me?" I asked, surprised. I had assumed that Mrs. Li and

the family were going on an extravagant picnic or visiting Aunt Xue or some other rich cousins' mansion. "Where? Why?"

"It's the first of the month, stupid!" Bisi said. "You may have gotten all those fancy lessons and learned to read, but you're still not very smart. They are taking us to the temple service, of course."

"But the Temple of Longevity is not hours—" I began.

"We're not going to the Temple of Longevity," Bisi said with exasperation, but I could see that her frustration was more about the inconvenience than it was for me. "We're off to the Infinite Stream Temple this time."

"That huge gold temple by the ocean?" I said. "Why?"

"For FuDing, of course," Shuwan said. "Mrs. Li hopes she can get the abbot to be a matchmaker for him. Infinite Stream Temple! That's why it has so much money—it gets an infinite stream of bribes."

"She'll need an elephant's weight of gold to get a matchmaker for FuDing," Bisi grunted. "No matchmaker is going to arrange a marriage with a well-born girl to that rice bucket. You'd think Mrs. Li would know that."

"She does. Mrs. Li is no fool! Why do you think—" Shuwan stopped, and both servants looked at me oddly.

"What?" I asked. As the silence grew longer, I put down the teapot I was washing and glared at them. "What?" I demanded. "Tell me!"

"By the time FuDing was seven, everyone knew he was a

brute as well as an idiot," Shuwan said. "And Mrs. Li knew that he might have a hard time finding a bride. . . ."

"Why do you think Mrs. Li was so desperate for you, the granddaughter of a scholar?" Bisi said. "She could've gotten any peasant's kid for cheaper and without any silly promises. She wanted a girl of good blood, just in case."

I stared. If Mrs. Li couldn't find a suitable bride, I was going to have to marry FuDing? Me? I felt as if I had eaten spoiled fish.

"You're not marrying age yet," Shuwan said, trying to be kind. "You have a couple of years. That's why Mrs. Li is trying to find FuDing a bride now. She's hoping she can get someone else to marry FuDing before you have to."

"Though I'd say that's a pretty bleak hope!" Bisi sniffed.

I thought of FuDing and his hairy fingers that were too clumsy to hold a paintbrush but so adept at torturing bugs. If I had listened more carefully, would I have heard their silent screams? Tears of horror filled my eyes.

Shuwan heaved an impatient sigh. "You made her cry again!" she complained.

"Well," Bisi retorted, "at least this time she's got a good reason."

The next morning, the streets around the House of Li overflowed with servants, horses, and sedan chairs. Mrs. Li's chair was so large that it needed four men on either side to carry it. FuDing's was not as large, but he was so heavy that the same number of men were needed to carry him. Then the cousins and aunts filled the carriages, and the horses were burdened with the supplies and gifts. Shuwan, Bisi, and I were to share a donkey, with the agreement that we would take turns riding, even though I had doubts about when my turn would be.

"It's sheer craziness!" Shuwan grumbled as we paraded past the gawking neighbors, most of them awed by the grandness of our procession. "Going to that ocean temple carrying chests of jade and strings of cash! We'll be prime targets for robbers. I wouldn't be surprised if pirates docked their boats just to raid us."

I remembered Shuwan's fear of pirates.

"Weren't some pirates seen recently?" I asked slyly. "I think someone said it was the Red Flag Fleet."

"I hope not!" Shuwan said with such fear that I felt a little bad for teasing her. "They are the worst! No one can stop the Red Flag Fleet!"

"The Imperial Navy has tried three times to capture them," Bisi said helpfully, "but failed each time. I heard that the Emperor has even offered amnesty to the captain and the crew if they'd agree to retire."

"Why would they retire?" Shuwan said. "They take what they want, and no one can stop them. And here we're going with all our gold! We might as well be throwing it into the ocean for them."

The trip to Infinite Stream Temple was a long one, but enjoyable. My turn to ride the donkey came much sooner than I had expected, for my short legs could not keep up with the procession, and Shuwan was ordered to allow me to ride so that I wouldn't slow down the group. She did this begrudgingly, until it was discovered that because I was so small, the donkey could bear the weight of another. So I rode along merrily, enjoying Shuwan and Bisi's bickering about who would ride with me.

And I marveled at all I saw. Even the scrubby, unkempt brush on the dirt road was a pleasure to see. Mrs. Li insisted that her residence be immaculate at all times. Even stray leaves had to be plucked from the paths of the garden. (I knew this because clearing the walkways was one of my jobs.)

But the sea was what mesmerized me. It whispered with a quiet thunder, and when I saw the "waves made of dragon scales," just like in one of Li Po's poems, I gasped.

However, after "thirty-six twists and turns of the valley," the Infinite Stream Temple came into view. High on a rocky hill, it was impossible to miss, for even from a distance the temple was a brilliance of gold. The temple's bright yellow and red walls and roofs dazzled, a loud, vibrating blare among the soft grays and silvers of the landscape.

"If I were a pirate," I said, "I'd raid that temple myself."

"Shut up about pirates already!" Shuwan snapped.

I grinned and our procession began along the path toward the temple. As the donkey climbed I heard the murmur of the sea, as if it were sighing a secret, and turned to look down at it. From my seat on the donkey, I could see the expanse of the ocean—the rolling waves glistening like silver folds of silk embroidered with threads of . . . red? I straightened. Unmoving and still, a dozen large junks sat in the water, the masts red-wrapped spikes stabbing into the sky, as if waiting. Waiting for what? Their captain and crew? But the only seamen who would dare raise a crimson sail were the Red Flag Fleet pirates! I scanned the shoreline below and stared at the sampans—fifty of them, or maybe even a hundred, all piled together like discarded shoes in the sand. As one stray sampan began to bob away, I felt my own thoughts lurch. There were pirates here!

"Bisi," I said, grabbing her arm. "Pirates!"

"Stop teasing Shuwan." Bisi shook me off. "You little brat, you think you're so funny. . . ."

But her voice trailed off as hundreds of screams echoed from the front of the procession. Servants, silk, and sedans seemed to fly toward me, and I felt Bisi throw herself from the donkey, shoving me face-first onto the ground. Something hard hit the back of my head, but before all became black, I knew that the Li family had reached the doors of the temple and had been welcomed in by the pirates.

I dreamed I was a small child, being rocked gently in a mother's arms. "Shhh," she whispered in my ear. "Shhh . . ."

"Is that one awake yet?" a rough voice said.

My eyes flew open. The soft rocking had been caused by the waves of the sea, and the ocean's roar had been the whisper. I sat up and saw a splash of red against blue—an unfurled sail against the sky. I was on a pirate boat!

"Now she is!" another voice hooted.

A forest of men stood before me, but beneath the raucous laughter, I heard sniffling. I looked and saw Bisi next to me, whimpering like a puppy.

"This was supposed to be a grab-and-go!" a man said. "The captain's not going to like seeing these prisoners."

"Indeed," a low voice behind me said as all the men immediately quieted. "She does not."

The captain was a woman? She strode forward, and it was then that I saw Tianyi, the captain of the Red Flag Fleet, the most feared pirate of the sea.

I could only gape. Teacher had once told me about the powerful goddess Xi Wangmu and how she was sometimes described as ferocious and terrible, having the claws and teeth of a tiger and the tail of a panther. But she was also described as being incredibly lovely and the Queen of the Heavens. I had protested at the conflicting descriptions. I had thought it impossible for one to be so beautiful and so fierce at the same time, but as I gazed at Tianyi, I suddenly understood. Her black silk hair billowed like the sails behind her, and her eyes sparkled like black coals ready to flame.

"Well, Weigu?" Tianyi said, and I saw the pirate actually whiten.

"I thought maybe that one could be ransomed," the pirate named Weigu replied, nodding toward me. "That family had a child, right? I thought maybe this one was it."

Tianyi gave me a quick glance and made a sound of annoyance.

"Stupid donkey! Look at her! Are those the clothes of someone from a rich family?" she said. She grabbed my hands and thrust them in the pirate's face. "Look at these hands! These are the hands of a servant! There's no ransom here! Idiot!"

The pirate cowered as Tianyi looked around. "And what straw bag grabbed her?" she said, nodding toward Bisi.

"Dihan took her," one of the men said. "He thought she was pretty."

"Did he?" Tianyi said dangerously. She drew her sword and walked to a man, placing her sword at his neck. "If you tried to spoil her, I'll cut your head off."

"I didn't!" the man protested. "I promise!"

"I know," Tianyi said with a sweet smile, putting her sword away. "That's why I'm not going to."

"I thought . . . you know how the Po Tsai pirates asked us for a woman to trade, and we owe them for that fight with the Imperial Navy when our other ships were late and . . . and . . . ," Dihan began to stammer.

Tianyi looked at Bisi—even with her nose red from crying she did look rather nice—and contemplated. For a brief moment, I saw Tianyi's eyes flash with pity.

"Too plain," Tianyi said, looking away. She tossed her hand. "They won't want her."

"Too plain?" Dihan asked. "That's what you said last time!"

"Do you think I cannot judge a woman's beauty?" Tianyi said, taking a step toward him. Like Weigu, Dihan cringed. "Give them enough cash to return and we'll drop them off at the next port." Then, throwing Dihan a cold glance, she added, "Perhaps we should have *your wife* help you bring them to shore."

"Please!" I was shocked to hear my own voice. "Don't send me back."

Everyone looked at me in astonishment, and I could not blame them. But even though the words had spilled out of me without thought, I suddenly found that I truly meant them. What did I have to return to? Being bossed by everyone, scrubbing chamber pots, and marrying FuDing? I shuddered at the thought.

But Tianyi had already dismissed me. "This is a pirate ship, not a nursery," she said. Then, addressing the crew, she ordered, "Bring up the rest of the loot!"

I bowed my head, surprised by the tears that filled my eyes. Bisi hissed a stream of insults at me, which, after years of practice, I easily ignored. Instead, after wiping my eyes, I found myself fascinated as the men threw the chests and packages from the sampans in such a well-practiced rhythm that it seemed to match the movement of the waves.

But not perfect. "Hey! Dumb melon!" shouted a pirate as another fumbled with a crate of tea bricks. It splashed into the water.

"Ohh!" I groaned. "And that was Iron Goddess tea!"

I had spoken aloud, thinking no one was listening to me. But Tianyi had the ears of a tiger and turned at my words. "How do you know that was Iron Goddess tea?" she demanded.

"It said so," I answered. "On the label."

"And this batch here," she said, pointing to another tea brick. "Is this Iron Goddess, too?"

"No," I said. "It says 'Mountain Silver Needle tea.' "

Tianyi tore open the package, broke off some leaves in her hands, and smelled the tea. She looked at me carefully, her eyes piercing. "Come with me," she ordered.

She led me into the captain's quarters, where I gazed around with great interest. It was a room of luxury—lavish silks draped over plush cushions, an intricately carved sandalwood bed, and red lanterns. In the entrance, two small wooden soldiers stood guard in front of a shrine that housed a goddess carved of ivory, surrounded by marigolds.

Tianyi motioned me to sit, and I watched curiously as she pulled out a wooden chest, plain and uncarved.

"Long ago, we raided a passenger ship. While all the wealthy nobles threw their goods at us and begged for mercy, one man jumped in front of this chest and grabbed a sword," Tianyi said. "He held the sword as if it were a broomstick, and it was easy to see he was no match for even the smallest of my men. But he fought valiantly to protect his treasure." Her face softened at the memory. "I would have spared him for that, but he was mortally wounded."

Tianyi worked the chest's clasp as she continued. "As he fought, I wondered what treasure he had that was so valuable. And when he died, I found it was this."

She opened the chest and I gasped. Books! Hundreds of books! I put my hands on them reverently. *Poems of Li Po. The Classic of Music. Spring and Autumn Annals.*

"Can you read these?" Tianyi asked me.

I nodded.

She looked at me, her eyes sparkling with an inner fire. "Teach me," she said, "and you can stay."

So I did.

* * *

Now, as I write this on a pirate ship whose red sails paint the sky, I ride the vast ocean. The wind is wild, and the waves are endless, and the shore is so distant it is hard to imagine that it even exists. But my head is raised and I can't help but smile. For while the path before me might be difficult, it will be my own.

Sol Painting, Inc.

MEG MEDINA

I reach inside the window of Papi's van and yank on the handle to open the passenger door. It's my turn to ride in front. Roli sat there last time.

"You think they'll need a painter soon?" Papi asks as I slide in next to him.

I follow his gaze to the second floor of building twenty-two. Men dressed like astronauts are tossing furniture into tall canisters marked BIOHAZARD. Doña Rosa, one of the old ladies who lived over there, died in her living room last week. Her TV was on, so no one knew anything was wrong for two whole days. That means we were all sleeping near a corpse. A shiver runs through me every time I think about Doña Rosa's ghost hovering in the halls, insulted that no one noticed she was dead.

"If they do, I'm out," I say. For starters, Doña Rosa was mean enough when she was alive. Who in their right mind wants to risk meeting her now that she's a spirit nursing a grudge? "I'm not going in there."

"Why not?"

"She's scared of putrefaction." Roli climbs into the back of the van and parks himself on one of Papi's paint buckets. My brother likes to show off his big science words, almost as much as he likes showing off his biceps, especially in front of Papi, who wants him to be a doctor. "That means human rot."

"I *know* what it means," I lie. "But that's not the reason."

"Are you afraid of ghosts?" Roli makes his best zombie face and holds up his hands like claws. "Ooooooooh . . ."

"Have some respect for *los muertos,* Rolando," Papi says, trying not to laugh. He crosses himself and starts to back out of the space.

I give Roli a stony look. He's right, but I know better than to let him know I'm scared. So I turn back to Papi.

"I'm too busy, that's all. School starts next week, and I have to finish my summer reading." I root inside the bakery bag for my *pan Cubano.* I take a deep breath of the warm bread that's dripping in butter and grilled flat the way Roli and I like it. I tear off a chunk and sink my teeth in. A full mouth will keep me from lying any more than necessary.

Papi smiles at me and pulls the bill of my painter's cap down over my eyes. "I can't argue with making a good start at your new school, so I'll let you off this time. But don't get used to it. You wanted to be my number one apprentice, remember?"

"Mmmm," I say, nodding.

Papi and I have a long-term business plan. I'm going to take over his company one day and turn it into an empire. Home Depot will eat my dust. I've already designed my business cards. They've got a sun rising and fancy gold letters: MERCI SUAREZ, CEO, SOL PAINTING, INC.

Roli makes a face and snatches the bag from me. He knows I haven't cracked open a single book on my summer reading list, but at least he doesn't say so. In fact, I think he felt bad for me, because he loaned me his good earbuds and CD player. Audiobooks to the rescue. He did the calculations while we were checking them out of the library. "You'll be done in a mere thirty-four hours."

Roli starts telling Papi about the process of human decomposition after death and proper biohazard cleanups, so I tune him out. This is definitely the dark side of having a science geek for a brother. Not that it's ever been easy. Even when he was younger, Roli liked to dissect salamanders, dead roaches, and other creepy things. He always wanted to play Operation, too—which would have been fun except that he changed the rules. You had to name the body parts correctly. "No, not the Adam's apple," he'd say as I tweezed out a piece without making the buzzer sound. "It's the *laryngeal prominence*. Say it or it doesn't count." Geez, you'd think he would have pity on somebody who was five. But no, Roli never cut me a break.

Anyway, these days Roli likes crime shows almost as much as he likes science. He says he's going to be a medical examiner. Poking around dead bodies all day? No thank you.

The air conditioner in Papi's truck is shot, so I lean my head out the window. Even with the windows open, I'm sweating in my long overalls. I've lived in West Palm Beach my whole life, but even I can't stand it here in August. It's 7 a.m. and we're already at 85 degrees, if the frog thermometer at my bedroom window is right.

Papi looks over at me and grabs my arm. "¡Ay! Don't lean on the door. The latch is loose. Your mother will kill me if you fall."

I scoot over.

"They sent our school schedules," Roli says, licking his greasy fingers. "Mine is sweet. I've got Microbiology first thing in the morning."

Oh, good. A whole year of listening to him talk about germs. I just survived his year in chemistry. For two solid semesters he asked for things by their chemical formula, just to annoy me. "I'd like a glass of H-two-O, please. Pass the sodium chloride for my french fries. This banana bread could use more sucrose."

I close my eyes, listening. Blah-blah, science club, blah-blah, college application.

I wonder what it's going to be like for *me* this year. Roli and I will both be at Seaward Pines, although I'll be in the lower school with all the other seventh-grade "amoebas" (his word). Roli is five years older than I am—a senior. The last time we were in the same school, I was in kindergarten and he was one of the bossy safety patrols with a plastic badge. After that, he became a Sunshine Scholar at fancy Seaward Pines School, where everybody thinks he's a genius.

Mami says I'm going to love Seaward Pines, but I don't know. I'm not much for fancy, and everything about that place is shiny and stiff. Even the red blazers I'll have to wear look hot and silly, if you ask me. Plus, no one from our neighborhood goes there, except Roli, so I'll have to make new friends. Stuff like that doesn't bother Roli. In fact, he's never brought home a friend in all the years he's gone there. I asked him about it once, but he told me to close my oral cavity.

I think what Mami really means is that *she's* going to love it. Last year was tough on her. My highest grade was a C, as in "*Caramba, niña,* what are you doing? You're shaming us!" Well, it was frustrating for me, too. To think, all my years of perfect attendance and neat penmanship did absolutely nothing to butter up my teachers at report-card time. It's what we call a poor return on investment in the business world. Mami finally said, *"¡Hasta aquí!"* and called Papi to "discuss my future," so I knew I was dead meat. I fought it as best I could, but they decided that I needed "a more structured learning environment," aka Seaward Pines.

"Why does it matter if I get an A in science or English?" I cried to Mami. "I'm going to take over Papi's business anyway!"

She gaped at me like a fish out of water. "Business? Is that what you're calling a dented van and the few guys who show up when they feel like it? A *business*?"

Mami: She has no vision. No wonder she and Papi don't get along.

Anyway, with Roli's help, I managed to broker a deal. I agreed not to run away. I'd go to Seaward Pines but *only* if I could apprentice with Papi—and get paid. So far, they're living up to the agreement. I'm twelve, so for now, I mostly do the trim, and I'm not allowed to go on all the jobs on account of child labor laws and all that bull. I've been on two sites so far: Ramon's Auto Parts (not bad since it was air-conditioned) and the marina, which left me smelling like bait for days.

"So, I have a surprise today," Papi says.

I study him. This could be bad. Among my parents' past surprises: "We've decided to get divorced."

46

"You're taking us to the science museum instead of to a job site?" Roli says hopefully. I roll my eyes. What an attitude. When I'm in charge, he'll be the first one to go.

"No, but you're close." Papi sticks his arm out to make a turn signal and heads over the bridge toward Palm Beach. "It's about the job."

I sit up and look outside, realizing he hasn't told us where we're working today. "Where's the site?" I ask.

The whole sky reflects in Papi's paint-speckled shades as he looks over and smiles. "Guess."

I look around for a clue. The Intracoastal twinkles beneath us as we cross the bridge into Palm Beach. The houses on this side of the canal are large, and they have bougainvillea vines trailing from their balconies. Royal palms line the street that ends at the ocean. Papi makes one turn after another on the quiet side streets where fancy cars are parked in the driveways and nannies push strollers in the shade.

Maybe we'll be painting one of the big mansions? I could run into one of the rich tycoons who live here and run a few business ideas past him. . . .

Roli crowds into the front seat to look at where we are, too. "Where *are* we going?"

"Move back," I say. He's breathing in my ear, and he hasn't brushed his teeth.

"No guess yet?" Papi asks.

Then the stone archway of Seaward Pines School appears up ahead. We drive past the perfectly manicured front lawn, startling a flock of ibises as we go. A team of men in wide-brimmed hats is running weed whackers and mowers.

"What are we doing here?" I ask.

Papi maneuvers us around back to the service entrance near the fields and parks in a spot reserved for maintenance crews. When he shuts off the engine, the van shudders to silence.

"I did a trade for your tuition," he says, turning to us. "We paint the gym and a few classrooms, and it won't cost me *un centavo* to have Merci attend this semester! *¿Qué te parece?* Your old man is always thinking!" He taps his temple and grins.

Roli glances at me uneasily and then shrinks into his seat again. "You should have told us," he mumbles. Something in his voice sounds tight, faraway.

But Papi doesn't hear him over the *squuuuueeeaaak* of the van door.

"Let's go, Team Suarez," he says.

I hop out and start gathering the drop cloths and extenders from the back. I already know where the gym is; we came here for Orientation Night last spring. If I remember, the place is humongous. We could be here for days. Maybe I'll ask for a raise.

"Are you going to help or what?" I ask Roli. "These paint cans are heavy, you know."

He doesn't answer.

Finally, Papi looks up. He stares at Roli for a second before climbing in to help me with the cans. Papi can carry several cans in each hand. He's the strongest dad I know. Wiping the sweat from his forehead, he points across the grass. "Follow those signs to the main office," he says. "Tell them we're here."

I start down the path, dodging the sprinklers and hopping over the bricks with people's names chiseled into them.

"*Vamos,* Roli," I hear Papi say.

Mrs. McDaniels, head secretary, wears high heels and clear nail polish. Everything on her desk is dangerously neat, so I can see she's the prickly type. She might even be an enforcer, so I'll have to keep my eye on her this year. Uniform length, the shine in your shoes, standard-issue headbands. You name it, she'll regulate it. I can feel her eyes on my head, so I pull off my cap. (No hats in school, according to the sign.) Naturally, my thick hair goes *boing.*

"Sol Painting at your service," I say, sticking out my hand. "I'm Merci." I put one of Papi's business cards on the counter.

She smiles cautiously and studies the card. "Aren't you a little young to be working?"

"The rest of the crew is outside, ma'am." It pays to be professional, even with annoying customers. "We're ready to start on the gym."

The phone rings.

I glance around uncomfortably as she explains that the head of school is at a meeting. The leather furniture makes it feel like a doctor's office in here. There are oil pastel portraits behind acrylic cases, and photographs of a group of students at the Great Wall of China.

Mrs. McDaniels hangs up and closes one of the enormous files sitting on her desk. I try to catch the name on the tab as she looks for the master keys, but it's too far away. My folder could be in this stack, but I don't say so. You never know what's in your permanent record. *Height: four eleven. Prone to daydreaming and lost assignments.*

She comes to the counter and looks down at me carefully. Finally, she slides a binder at me.

"Sign in," she says. "The time is exactly seven-forty-three."

Roli and Papi are waiting in the shade outside the gym when we arrive a few minutes later. The paint supplies are piled at their feet.

"Good morning," Mrs. McDaniels says to Papi as she walks past him. Maybe she's not so observant after all. Roli is standing right there. You'd think she'd say hello to one of their A students, but maybe she doesn't recognize him in overalls.

She throws open the door for us and switches on the overhead lights. "Be sure to mark the work area. We don't want any of the students tripping on a drop cloth and having an accident." I can practically see the thought bubble over her head. *Paperwork*.

She turns on her heels and clicks away up the path.

"Who's here?" I ask after she's gone. It's not like Seaward Pines has summer school. There's no such thing as failing here. Roli told me you're just "disappeared" back to your home school. I picture kids vaporizing, leaving behind their red blazers in heaps.

Roli shifts on his feet and points across the fields. Beefy football players are doing drills. Nearby, the girls' soccer team is practicing their passes. If you listen hard, you can hear the coaches' whistles, the grunts as the teams knuckle down.

I inch up the path a bit. I love soccer—and I'm good. Papi taught me most of my moves. He plays on a Sunday *fútbol* league at the park when his knees aren't bad—and thanks to the dads on the team, I know how to dribble and stall the ball on my ankles like a pro. Every once in a while, if they're short, they let me play keeper. I'm almost never stuck on the sidelines blowing a stupid *vuvuzela*.

Maybe we can sit in the shade and watch for a while to see if they're any good? All employees are entitled to breaks, aren't they? But when I turn to ask Roli, he's gone.

"Get to work," Papi says. He's already inside, spreading the drop cloths.

* * *

Seaward's school colors are red and gray, so all the doors and baseboards are the searing color of a fire engine. Every time I shift my eyes to the floor, I see globs of blue and green floating in front of me, like levitating beach balls.

"Hey! I'm having those afterimages," I say to Roli. He's the one who explained to me how the cone cells in your eyes work. It's kind of cool to be blind for a few minutes.

"Hurry up, Merci. I want to get out of here." He dips his roller again and turns back to the wall. His muscles strain against his T-shirt as he rolls faster and faster. "It shouldn't take forever to paint a stupid door."

"It does if you're doing a good job," I say.

I stand up and look over at Roli. What a disaster. When Papi sees this, he's dead. Papi says a good painter can work without splatters or drips. Roli has sloshed paint all over the place, and there are streaks and drips on the walls where there shouldn't be any. No quality control, that's the trouble. I'll have to discuss this with Papi as we determine Roli's future with us.

"You guys ready to take a break?" Papi calls. He's across the gym, patching a hole in the drywall. "We can take a ride to Burgers and Shakes."

We usually pack our lunch and dine "alfresco," as Papi calls it, which just means we picnic under a tree. It's too hot today, though, and a chocolate shake sounds like heaven.

I'm about to put down my brush when the door I've been painting swings wide open. Light floods inside and makes me squint. A group of upper-school girls is clustered outside. Their sweaty faces are almost as red as the paint. Grass clippings cling to their shin guards.

They're jostling and shouting.

"It's boiling!"

"Go in already."

"Stop shoving!"

"I have to pee!"

A tall girl stands in the lead. She's probably the team captain, if that *C* on her jersey means anything. Plus, she looks the part, with muscular legs and hair piled high on her head like a lopsided doughnut. Before I can stop her, she reaches her arms wide and grabs the wet doorframe as if she's trying to keep her flock from moving forward.

She pulls her hands back when she realizes what she's done.

"Damn!" She stares at her palms, then gives me an ugly look, like it's my fault.

One of the girls next to her giggles. "Oops."

I rub my eyes with my forearm, trying to see them better around the big green globs that still linger before my eyes. I'm positive I stuck a sign in the grass outside, just like Papi said. WET PAINT. USE OTHER DOOR. But even if they missed it, couldn't they see that the surface is shiny? Can't they smell the fumes or see me standing here with a paintbrush? Hello?

I'm furious, but my tongue goes thick in my mouth. Maybe it's the girl's bright eyes on me or maybe it's that they're all older. You have to be in high school to play on the varsity team, right? Or maybe it's really because Roli doesn't turn and come to help me. He keeps his back to them and keeps painting.

Thank goodness for Papi. He wipes his hands and starts walking toward them from across the gym. He has a quick temper, so I'm expecting him to make a fuss the way he does at Roli and me when we track in dirt or argue too much. Or else he might just freeze them with his look, which is almost as bad. Papi's a big guy, and his eyes can go narrow and dark when he's mad.

But before Papi can reach them, the girls start shoving again, trying to get out of the heat. They don't seem to care that he's holding up his hand to wave them off. It's like they don't see him at all.

"Move!"

"Let us in, Catie!"

And just like that, they burst through, their hands and bodies sliding over the wet door as I stand there, rooted to the spot. They barrel through, shrieking with laughter as they get smeared. One or two make handprints on each other's backs. And then somebody wipes herself clean on one of the walls Roli finished a while ago. I stare, breathless, at the long streak of red fingers along the length of it.

They're dead—and I can't wait to see it happen. Papi is going to yell at them for ruining my work. Any second, his voice will boom across the gym. The walls will rattle. When Papi loses his temper, it feels as if you're trapped inside a huge storm cloud.

But as the seconds tick by, absolutely nothing happens. I finally turn to see that Papi has stopped in his tracks, his hands in his pockets as he watches the girls race past. We are ghosts as they go by—unseen. Finally, the tall girl looks at us from the top of the steps leading to the locker room.

"*Perdón*," she calls out in a heavy American accent before she takes the steps, two at a time. There's laughter, hoots. Then another voice calls out from somewhere, "Excuse-oh *moi*!"

A metal door slams behind them.

I feel like I've been slapped. An ugly coldness creeps up from my stomach as we stand there in silence. *Perdón? Excuse-oh moi? Do they think we don't speak English? And even if we didn't, would that make their silly apology any better?*

But it's Papi's stillness that makes me feel worse. *Why didn't he say anything? He's Papi. He's the boss, an adult, the guy in charge. How could he let this happen?*

It's only when a man with sweat stains around his armpits comes jogging to the door that the silence is broken. It's Mr. Falco, the guidance counselor. He spoke last year at one of the parent college nights I was dragged to. Seaward Pines School was a special place, he said that night. A school with a history of turning out fine young men and women.

He steps carefully through the door, looks at the mess, and shakes his head.

"I told them to use the side entrance," he says, sighing.

"They should come clean it up," I snap.

Papi shoots me a warning look. "Quiet, Merci." His eyes slice through me in a way I'm not expecting. But why? I'm not the one who made this mess.

"But, Papi—"

"*Sio—*" he hisses.

When I drop my stare down at my shoes, he turns back to Mr. Falco and pastes on a smile. "It's no problem, sir. They're children, and accidents happen. We'll clean it up."

With those words, my father shrinks before my very eyes. My arms hurt, and I'm thirsty and hot. I feel ugly. My cheeks burn as I stand there, humiliated for all of us.

I will not *clean this up,* I tell myself. I slide my gaze to Roli. His jaw twitches as he rolls on a new coat of paint, but he won't look at me.

"Thank you," Mr. Falco says. He walks away and closes the glass door of the athletics office at the far end of the gym.

* * *

It doesn't take that long to touch up the walls or to repaint the door, but I'm furious just the same. I don't speak to Papi for the rest of the day, not even when he buys me an extra large chocolate shake. That afternoon, I let Roli sit in front and brood all the way home as I pick the dried red paint from under my nails. Every bump makes the springs in the seats squeak as we make one turn after another and head over the bridge again toward home. A million thoughts bang around inside my head, but I can't seem to turn them into a single question. All I feel is a rotting feeling inside. It's like I'm putrefying, just like Doña Rosa.

Finally, Emerald Isle Condominiums comes into view.

"I'll see if one of the guys from the team can help me finish up tomorrow," Papi says as Roli and I climb out. He doesn't look at me as he says it, which makes me feel satisfied. At least he knows I'm not speaking to him. He taps his horn before he pulls away, and Roli turns. "Make sure Merci works on her reading." Then he's off.

"I don't need your help," I hiss at Roli as the van disappears around the corner.

"Suit yourself," he says.

I don't follow Roli upstairs. Instead, I walk toward the pool. The old ladies who usually bob in the water aren't here. They might have been scared away by the heat, or maybe they're praying for Doña Rosa at the funeral parlor in Lake Worth. I let myself in the gate and sit at the pool's edge with my legs dangling in the water. Roli and I used to do handstands in here. We used to dive for pool sticks. But now all I see is an ugly pool. Leaves are floating on the surface, and I'm pretty sure there's a dead frog in the deep end. The deck chairs are lopsided, and the scummy water is warm enough to poach you. I think of the pretty office at Seaward Pines, the fountain with cherubs spitting water, and feel mad all over again.

I don't know how long I sit there, but finally, someone opens the gate behind me. "Mami says to come up." Roli has changed into shorts, and he's barefoot. "She wants you to eat."

"I'm not hungry." I go back to watching lizards dart around the pool deck.

Roli stays quiet for a few seconds. Then he walks over to where I'm sitting and curls his toes over the edge.

"Hunger strike, huh?" he says. "How long you think you'll hold out?"

I give him my darkest look.

Roli considers the water as a beetle paddles near our legs. He walks to the supply closet at the shallow end of the pool and finds the net. I watch him circle the perimeter, cleaning away the mess. He even scoops up the frog and hurls it like a lacrosse ball into the bushes. When he's done, he walks back to me. I can feel a fight between us.

"Merci . . . ," he begins.

But I strike first, hard and fast. "Seaward Pines is a dumb school," I blurt. "I'll hate it. And I hate Papi, too."

Roli sighs. He's quiet for a long while, which makes me uncomfortable. My brother has always been strangely good at reading my mind. Can't he see how awful it felt to be unimportant, to watch Papi stand there like a chump?

"What did you want Papi to do, Merci? Pitch a fit and blow your free ride?"

Without warning, tears spring to my eyes. He pretends not to notice. Instead, he cups my scalp with his enormous hand and gives a squeeze. "Try to let this idea into your thick cranium. Papi *chose* to be invisible today so you won't ever have to be."

I look up at him guiltily.

"That's harder to do than shooting off your mouth, Merci."

Without warning, he yanks off his shirt. He has Papi's same shape, even if he's a little skinnier. There are still tiny dots of paint in his hair, a smear at his elbow.

He cannonballs into the pool and makes a spray arc that soaks me to my underwear. For a second, I'm stunned. I want to shout at him, stay enemies, but instead, I take a deep breath and let the water offer what relief it will.

"Race?" He bobs back up to the surface, grinning. "Come on. Show me what you're made of."

I hesitate, my shame holding me still. But in the end, I stand up and shimmy out of my overalls until I'm just in a T-shirt and panties. I jump, arms wide, eyes open. Then I paddle after him, reaching and gasping into the deep end like mad.

Secret Samantha

TIM FEDERLE

It's a lot of pressure to pick a good elf name.

When I was little, I never stuck my pets with average names like Spot or Rover. It was more like Peanut Brittle or Sir Hop-a-Lot. But having to name *myself* for our Secret Santa week at school is *kind* of stressing me out—and it's almost my turn in the circle.

(I always seem to go last, which is just my luck.)

"Yoo-hoo, *Samantha*?" Miss Lee says.

Gah, I hate when people don't call me Sam, and it throws me off. I open my mouth, but my elf name doesn't come out the way I want it to. I want my elf name to be Flame, because I like the way fire changes from orange to blue to smoke, without even warning you.

"Um . . . Sparkles," I say.

"Sparkles?" Miss Lee asks, probably because my voice is so small.

"Yeah," I say. "Sparkles. The elf."

It's no Flame, but it seems safe enough.

Still, a few of the boys begin telling some kind of Sparkles-themed joke. They'll find anything to make fun of. Like when I said I wanted to be called "Sam" last year, and they all said, "Is that because you look like a *boy*?"

Maybe I should have expected it. I had really short hair then, which I'd begged my mom to let me get cut when we moved here. She warned me not to: "Kids can be cruel, honey," she said, and she was right. They called me Sam the Man.

Which doesn't even rhyme, by the way.

Anyway, I let my hair grow back out and I stopped telling people to call me Sam, and here we are.

"With Sparkles in the bag," Miss Lee says, picking up a Santa hat and walking into the center of our circle (after stepping over Parker's book bag), "we've got a room full of elves!" Miss Lee hops up and down, like we're five years old. "How fun was that?"

That's her signature phrase. Miss Lee taught the second graders last year, and all of her lessons feel too babyish for us sixth graders.

She parades the hat around, so we can pick out the name of the elf who we'll be the Secret Santa for. Right when it's my turn, someone notices that there's snow coming down, which isn't that rare of an occurrence in Pennsylvania. Still, snow is snow, and now Miss Lee has whisked the hat away and we're all pressing our noses against the freezing window and counting snowflakes.

That's when we feel a *whoosh,* the vacuum sound of Room 314's door opening.

The principal is here. Never good. She scrunches her face at all of us and shoots Miss Lee a glare.

"First snow of the year," Miss Lee says, stepping forward to defend her turf. Her pink heels shriek against the waxed linoleum. Miss Lee always wears pink. She's beautiful.

"It's just *snow,* kiddos," the principal says. I hate when grown-ups call us kiddos.

But then: "Well, I think it's awesome," says a new voice, coming from behind the principal.

The voice steps inside our classroom. "The *snow,* I mean. Is awesome," says this girl, who isn't in a uniform like the rest of us.

Who is a little shorter than I am.

Whose fingernails are painted black-*white*-black-*white,* every other one.

"I'm from California," she says, and offers us a thumbs-up. The room is so silent with staring that you can hear the old clock ticking. Five ticks later, the girl says: "Wow, you people are *quiet.*"

Uh, I didn't speak for an entire week when I first got to school, and I only came from across the state!

"This is the new girl," the principal announces. And I think she says her name, too, but I don't even hear it because I'm off in Sam Land, wondering if I could ever stop biting my nails long enough to paint them black.

But then I'm back in room 314, right as the principal is saying that we ought to treat the girl "just the exact same way you treat each other." Which seems like a funny thing to say, because as the principal is saying it, Kyle V. is punching Eliot's shoulder.

When the door clicks shut behind the principal, we let out a nervous group laugh, like we're bottles of pop that have been opened too fast.

"We were just in the middle of playing Secret Santa," Miss Lee says. Somehow that gets us all running back into formation, to stand on the frayed edges of a worn-out square of gray carpet. "We're picking names out of a hat, and at *some* point this week you'll deliver a secret gift—"

"That's under five dollars!" shouts Mia. She's the class treasurer and is mildly obsessed with money.

"Yes, thank you, Miss Santos," Miss Lee says, pausing before continuing her peppy explanation. Peppy would be a good elf name for Miss Lee. "And then on Friday, we'll all guess who's who, and—"

"Cool," says the new girl. "Got it."

She's still staring at the snow, but I can't stop staring at her.

Maybe it's because the rest of us look exactly alike. Same clothes, same haircuts, same hair *colors,* almost: a nothing-special brown like Peanut Brittle, the best ferret ever (may he rest in peace).

But this girl's clothes are sun-faded. This girl's hair is dark like a good secret. She looks like the kind of person who might get a tattoo someday. Like my aunt Hannah, in Ann Arbor.

"My goodness, I almost forgot!" Miss Lee says. "You have to assign yourself a cute elf name!"

I cringe for the new girl. This would all freak me out if it were *my* first day. But she doesn't even blink.

She's from California.

"For instance," Miss Lee says, "Kaylee is Sunshine, and Kyle H. is Slugger, and Aadhya is Mistletoe. So before you can play the game, I'll need you to—"

"Blade," the girl says.

"I'm sorry?"

On cue, a few of the boys begin telling Blade-themed jokes. But Blade looks at them like that one blank-faced emoji that doesn't have a mouth. And they stop.

"Blade is my elf name."

She steps farther into our circle, and I notice Blade's got on amazing military boots that are all scuffed up. Those won't be around past day one. We girls are required to wear Mary Janes.

"Well, then," Miss Lee says, not sounding peppy anymore. "Blade."

You can tell Miss Lee is bothered to have an elf called Blade on her watch, but that's not the important part.

The important part is that as I'm thinking how fun it will be to sled with my best friend, Henry, this weekend, and how excited I am to see Dad for Christmas, and mostly how *wicked* the new girl's boots are, at the very same time I reach into the hat and somehow pull out the name Blade.

The period bell goes off right as she and I lock eyes, tight like matching puzzle pieces, almost like she can tell I picked her.

Rumors spread in the lunch line like a common cold.

Blade has a knife collection. Blade has a pet snake. Blade has *three* pet snakes. Blade feeds her pet snakes live rats, which she personally catches in the attic . . . of her *haunted house*. And the most shocking rumor of all: Blade called her teachers by their *first names* at her old school in Berkeley.

"I'm telling you," Henry says, in between bites of chicken fingers. "Reagan said J. J. O'Reiley lives across the street from the new girl. Apparently, her family moved in over the weekend and they are super weird."

" 'Weird' can mean anything, Henry. Everyone calls *us* weird." I'm glancing around the cafeteria, swirling a tater tot in some Italian dressing, and feeling glad that nobody ever sits with me and Henry. I love having a big table to spread out my art notebooks and draw. I don't even care if Henry spills various sauces on my drawings, which he *always does,* because then I turn the sauce splotches into cartoon characters.

"Okay, *true,*" Henry says, "but I think this girl is, like, *genuinely* weird. Did you see her *boots*?"

Not only did I see them, I want a pair. "I think they're pretty wicked," I say, and I'm proud of myself. I said it loud enough for Henry to hear me the first time.

The monitor whistles. Lunch is almost up. We eat in twenty-two-minute marathon sessions, and I always walk into life science with a bellyache. But today I barely ate a thing.

"Well, whatever," Henry says, gulping his strawberry milk away in two chugs. "As long as you don't replace *me* as your number one friend."

"Aw, Henry," I say, standing with my tray to gather my notebooks. "I think of you as more of a *pet* than a friend."

He acts all offended, but then he does his famous baboon snort and we both laugh.

"If I'm your pet, then can I finish your tater tots?"

I hand over my tray and roll my eyes, but Henry's the

best—even if I can't quite trust him with the secret that I'm Blade's Santa. When Henry's got a secret to keep, he looks like he has to pee. Frankly, it's a liability.

"Gosh," he says, smacking his lips, "I would marry tater tots if I could."

The official bell goes off, and the whole cafeteria shrieks and groans—but nothing can get me down now. I've just got life science and then band practice and then Mom is taking me last-minute Christmas shopping for Aunt Hannah and Miss Lee.

And also, the new girl. Who I can't seem to stop thinking about.

The mall is a zoo, if the zoo forgot to build cages.

Half the shops are permanently closed, and the food court is a war zone. But after we pick up an Applebee's gift card for Miss Lee, Mom beelines straight for a boutique that's within the price range of our Secret Santa rules.

"What about *this,* Sammy?" she says, holding up a mini makeup kit that's right by the front of this quirky pop-up shop. Mom calls me Sammy because she knows I hate Samantha, and she knows I prefer Sam, and so Sammy is kind of "in the middle." We are working on being in the middle with one another.

"Maybe," I say, and Mom goes, "Speak up, Sammy," and I say, *"Maybe."*

That right there is a good example of me being in the middle, because I *wanted* to throw the makeup against the wall and shout, *"Blade doesn't need makeup to be cool!"*

"Well, I'll hold on to it," Mom says, making apology eyes at the cashier. "Unless you find something better."

But I don't find something better, is the problem. I go up and down the aisles, and I find things that *I* could use—like these turquoise dragon earrings that might distract people from my giant ears, or this mini embroidered DIVA pillow that would be a good bed for my bunny, Sir Hop-a-Lot—but none of it seems very *Blade.*

"Samantha?" I hear from the front. I'm allowed out of my mom's sight for about ten seconds for every year I've been alive.

As I'm shuffling back to her, I'm making note of the silver high heels she's got on that I know make her feet "scream." She always looks so dolled up but so *uncomfortable.* She's the very opposite of me. I'd rather be plain and *relaxed.* If I could wear sweatpants to church, I would. If I could buzz off my hair, I would. I'm serious!

"So?" Mom says, tapping the makeup kit against the counter. "Shall we?"

But then she gets a phone call from her boyfriend—I recognize the special ring—and she hands the cashier both of her credit cards, says, "One of those should work," and steps away to take Scott's call.

When the cashier asks me, "All ready to check out?"

that's the *very same moment* I spot these long black shoe-laces dotted with gray skulls, on sale in a wire basket beneath the register.

"These, too," I whisper, sliding the shoelaces on top of the makeup kit. The lady swipes Mom's first card and hands me back the makeup and the shoelaces in a little wax paper baggie, and winks at me. I stuff the bag into my pocket before Mom even realizes what I've done.

Merry Christmas.

The next morning as my bus is driving into the loop outside school, I see a dirty white Jeep pull up in front of us—even though parents aren't supposed to use the front drive till after eight.

Blade gets out of the Jeep! Because of *course* she'd have the type of family that drives her to school. An amazing thing happens next which is that Blade stands on the side-walk and waves and waves and blows a kiss (!) to whoever is driving the Jeep.

I stopped hugging Mom outside school about a month ago, after Quentin made fun of Taylor for kissing her mom's cheek before the autumn band concert.

But Blade is just waving and waving without a care in the world.

She catches me catching her, maybe because I've stood

up in my seat and pulled the window down and stuck my head out, which is crazy. It's freezing. People in the bus are yelling at me to shut it.

Hi, I mouth to Blade, and she mouths, *Hi,* back, and she's still waving, except now it's at me.

I pull out my Magic 8 Ball keychain, as a good-luck charm. The whole bus ride over, I asked it if I should give Blade the makeup kit or the shoelaces. But every single time it came out "hazy," like it didn't know the answer. Which is nuts. It knows the answer to everything. That's why it's magic.

Later, we all enter language arts with a degree of excitement we usually save up for recess. But Miss Lee seems overcast today. *She's not even wearing pink.* "I have bad news," she says. "It's about . . . Secret Santa."

"Is it *canceled*?" says Noelle. She's very serious about Christmas. Hello, her name.

"Well, it's not exactly canceled," says Miss Lee, as we all gather on the rug. "But it turns out I've broken some administrative rules by talking about 'Santa'—who, of course, isn't even real!"

I look at Blade. She's already looking at me. She smirks like she's got something hot in her mouth. This makes me smirk, too, even though I'll die if Secret Santa is ruined.

"Not everybody celebrates Christmas," Miss Lee says. She's digging a fingernail track up and down her black stockings. "So now we're going to call our game . . . Secret *Sharers*."

Everybody is quiet. Jasmine's stomach gurgles so loud that Ethan high-fives her, and then it's silent in room 314 for a bit longer, and Blade, of all people, says, "So, what's the bad news?"

Whenever Blade speaks up, my chest goes bah-*boom*, bah-*boom*. It's the weirdest thing. Like an allergic reaction.

"That *was* the bad news," says Miss Lee. Her eyes wander over to her beloved corkboard, which twinkles with holiday glitter. "That we have to call the game Secret Sharers now."

Kaylee says, "As long as we're all still giving gifts, I think we're fine, Miss Lee!" and Miss Lee looks so relieved I think she's gonna cry.

"Forget *giving* gifts," says Noah. "I can't wait to *get* mine!"

Miss Lee stands and so we all do, and as we head back to our desks, she says, "The rules stay the same! To be clever little ninjas, you'll need to deliver your gifts with *secrecy* this week!"

Noelle calls out (without even raising her hand), "You mean 'elves,' Miss Lee? Clever little *elves*?"

Miss Lee twists a ring around her finger. "We're calling

you ninjas now, sweetheart." And then she grabs a stack of papers and begins our lesson on adverbs.

When I get home from school it's more bad news.

Usually, Mom has a snack set out for me on the kitchen island, but instead of baby carrots and a granola bar, it's just the skull shoelaces—and a Post-it note that says, CALL ME AT WORK.

She's been going through my drawers again.

I check my cell and see that a text came in, also from Mom.

The text says, CALL ME AT WORK.

"I wouldn't have minded buying you those shoelaces, Samantha, but you didn't ask," Mom says, when I've got her on the phone. "You've been sneaking around so much lately—and you don't even own boots!"

That reminds me to kick off my Mary Janes, which is the best part of every day.

"You stepped away to talk to Scott in the store," I say, "and I wasn't thinking."

It's a dangerous move to bring up Scott, because Mom knows I actually *like* this guy. He thinks I'm an ace cartoonist.

"Well, next time you want something, all you have to do is say so," Mom says in her distracted voice. I can hear her clicking away on the keyboard at her real estate office. "For the record, when *I* was in sixth grade I definitely would've preferred eye shadow over shoelaces. But it's a new generation, I guess." *Clickety-click-click.* "I'll return whichever gift you don't give her."

"*Mmkay,*" I say, and then Mom's cell phone rings at work, so I go, "Take that call!" and she says, "Hey—love you, Sam."

Five minutes later I've spread my art notebooks all over the kitchen table when it hits me that Mom called me Sam. Which makes me grin so hard that I snag a lip on my braces, and I don't even care.

Priorities: I take out my freshest green marker and try to draw Blade a good homemade card to go along with her shoelaces. But my Christmas trees are lopsided and my bubble letters are a joke.

Typical Tuesday.

So I text Henry, *wanna come over for a snack my mom made cupcaaaakes last night,* and both of his dads say it's okay, and literally only twenty minutes later he has provided me with an accidental vanilla frosting smear across a black sheet of construction paper.

It's going to make an amazing snowman.

I give in and tell Henry that I'm Blade's Santa. Saying her elf name out loud makes her . . . real. (It also makes my chest go bah-boom *and* my left thumb twitch. As if the allergic reaction is spreading.)

"You didn't sign the card," Henry points out. His chin is a cupcake disaster zone.

I write, *To Blade! From, GUESS WHO,* and I fold the card into an origami rabbit (my specialty), which reminds me that I have to feed Sir Hop-a-Lot. And so I do.

Then Henry and I wrap the skull shoelaces in an old *Calvin and Hobbes* cartoon, which is a big deal.

Calvin and Hobbes is my favorite.

The week goes on with barely any more snow. Which, *boo.*

But one nice thing is: in homeroom on Wednesday, Abby and Reagan *and* Parker separately ask me to be their gift deliverer, because I'm "so secretive."

Which I didn't even know about myself.

Another funny thing is: Abby got Reagan as an elf and Reagan got Abby, by coincidence. And Abby bought Reagan this lip gloss that changes color depending on your mood, and Reagan bought Abby this *ring* that changes color depending on your mood. Crazy, right?

Wednesday during lunch I leave the lip gloss in Reagan's cubby, and she squeals when she finds it. And then on Wednesday afternoon I'm alone in the back hallway, by the emergency exit, and I see my next chance. I tape the mood ring to Abby's locker, but when I back away I hear a raspy California voice say, "You are *sneaky.*"

It's Blade. I get stupid. "I'm not Abby's Santa!" I say.

Which is a catastrophe. I should be playing it cool, but I'm useless when caught. "I'm just a delivery elf!"

"Uh, don't you mean *ninja*?" Blade says, and I give her a *huh?* look and she goes: "Elves are outlawed around these parts, Sparkles."

Bah-*boom*. Twitch. Bah-*boom*. Twitch.

I can't tell if she's making fun of me, but then she says, "I'm *kidding*," and I giggle and pinch my elbow skin and look at anything but Blade's face.

That's when I notice she's got on standard-issue Mary Janes now. Just like the rest of us.

"Aren't those the worst?" I say.

She looks down and looks up and says, "I feel as if I'm wearing a costume." I giggle again, and then: silence.

The period bell goes off about a million hours later.

Blade says, "Social studies," I say, "Band practice," and we both make yuck faces before heading in opposite directions.

But I turn back around. "Is it true you have pet snakes?"

"Snakes" echoes in the hallway, which is impressive. If I'm known for anything, it's for how hard I am to hear. But my voice echoes three times: *snakes, snakes, snakes.*

She stands there looking at me like that one confused emoji. But then Blade smiles—I notice she's got braces, too—and goes: "If 'snakes' is the worst they're saying about me, that's pretty good."

Which isn't exactly a no.

"Cool," I say. And then: "I have a rabbit and I used to have a ferret!"

She gives me the thumbs-up before jutting it down the hall. "Social studies," she says again, and off she disappears.

It dawns on me, fifteen minutes later in the middle of band practice, that Blade must have been wearing color-changing lip gloss, because as we were hanging out back there discussing ninjas and Mary Janes and snakes, her smile went from green to purple.

On Thursday morning I wake up in a sweat, and I *hate* sweating, which is why Henry and I always *walk* the mile in gym class.

I didn't sleep well last night because of a nightmare. In it, I realized that if Blade was in fact wearing mood-change lip gloss, maybe she *is* a "makeup girl," after all. Maybe she'd prefer the makeup to the shoelaces for a present, which I'd planned to give her, at last, today.

When my alarm goes off I don't even hit snooze.

I run to my book bag and unwrap the skull shoelaces—carefully, because, duh, it's a *Calvin* strip and I don't want to tear through the punch line—and rewrap the paper around the makeup kit.

Mom asks me if anything is "up" at breakfast: "You didn't

even hit snooze," she says. But I go, "Nothing's up—I just want to get to school," and she looks at me like I'm a llama or a cactus or something, because I guess I've never said that before.

Language arts is my best chance to slip Blade her gift if I want to actually watch her open it—and I do!—but I'm scanning the room and there isn't a strong ninja candidate among *any* of these people.

All the boys except Ryan P. are *terrible* secret keepers, and Ryan P. is out today for personal reasons (the rumor in the halls was "lice"). And forget the other girls—they are a giant clique. Frankly, I still feel like the new girl, even with an *actual* new girl around.

So I do the unthinkable, right by the aquarium. I pull Miss Lee aside.

"Miss Lee, could you please, *um,* be my ninja?"

She does an ace job sneaking the makeup kit onto Blade's desk, because at one point during class Blade goes to the water fountain. When she gets back, I'm wiggling around in my seat so much that it makes the chair squeak.

Blade then does the cutest thing I've ever seen a non-kitten do: she takes my origami rabbit card and makes it "hop" across her desk, just for herself. And then she opens the card and her forehead goes red.

Then Blade picks up my gift and tears *right through* the *Calvin* cartoon.

And she dangles the makeup kit in the air like it's a snake. Like it's *three* scary snakes.

When Blade seems to realize that the whole class is staring at her, she makes the exact same face I make every year on my birthdays, right after Mom gives me a new dress or a perfume set.

Miss Lee asks us to take out our notebooks and turn to a blank page. But as I fumble beneath my desk for my book bag, a gift baggie falls from the top of it.

I had completely forgotten I was going to receive a present myself this week.

"Open it," somebody says.

Inside the baggie I discover a pink purse made of fake leather. It glimmers like a mermaid's tail. *A sparkle bag for Sparkles* is scribbled on a sheet of crumbly yellow paper.

And that's when I ask to go to the nurse's office, "for personal reasons." And I don't mean lice.

The nurse isn't sure what to do with me, and neither am I. I feel like I'm going to sneeze except instead of a sneeze it's crying. My temperature is fine, so the nurse gives me a lollipop, and paces.

Mom comes to see me at school—a first. "Sammy, why the tears, why the tears?" We have been working on me not crying so much, but as soon as I see her, I'm a goner.

"Nobody *gets* me," I say, and I hold up the pink purse as evidence.

I can't stop thinking about Abby and Regan and how they just *knew* that the other person would like mood-changing gifts. Basically everyone in my class got perfectly picked presents this week, but I didn't.

And neither did Blade. I saw it. I *felt* it. I know.

Mom gives me a big hug. The nurse leaves us alone on the cots.

"We've had a tough couple of years, and you are amazing to me," Mom says—and that should make me cry harder, but it stops my tears up like a bathtub plug.

"I am?"

"Yes! It's your first Christmas with Daddy and me being divorced, and you're still getting used to the new apartment, and it's been a lot for you. Frankly, it's been a lot for *me,* too. For us."

Her phone rings, and even though Mom's eyes flicker toward her own purse—which is also pink—she reaches in and silences the call. Which is ten kinds of great.

But the important part is that as she reaches into her purse, I see the skull shoelaces inside.

"Mom!" I say. "Can I have those shoelaces? *Please?*"

Mom looks thrown off. "Well, you caught me! I was heading to the mall to find you boots."

"Boots?"

"To go with the shoelaces!"

"Oh! Thank you! But they're not for me!"

"I'm confused."

"I have an idea of how to make today better," I say— because that's something Mom and I used to do when I'd cry: we'd make a list of five ways to make it better, and usually by the third way we'd found *the* way.

"O . . . kay?"

"But the idea needs shoelaces!" I say.

Mom pauses for two seconds that feel like forever. But then she hands me the laces and kisses my sweaty bangs and says, "Then I guess you'd better take them."

At lunch I commission Henry to wipe Cheeto crumbs across a crisp white piece of paper that I "borrowed" from the librarian's printer.

Then I draw a tiger tail on Henry's best thumbprint smear, using my trusty orange marker to re-create the torn *Calvin* comic. And then I wrap my new drawing around the skull shoelaces.

I can't stop thinking about how they'll look in Blade's

boots, on Blade's feet, on Blade's legs. Even though she's shorter than me she has the longest legs, I swear.

"Hobbes turned out great," Henry says. "One of your best."

I agree.

I finish off my tater tots and make a very bold decision just to hand the shoelaces to Blade myself. Bold, because it's illegal to reveal your true identity before tomorrow's Secret Sharers ceremony. But I am feeling bold. I have decided that the ongoing bah-*booms* and the twitches and the itchy feet (a new symptom) aren't an allergy, but a sign.

Henry wishes me luck, and we have an impromptu burping contest. I let him win.

Gym is awful, but I survive.

After gym I discover Blade at a drinking fountain, as predicted. She drinks a *lot* of water because California is going through a drought. She thinks it's amazing that water is unlimited in Pennsylvania.

"I was sort of looking for you," I say. "Here." I hand her the shoelace package. "It's my backup gift for you." I look at the ceiling. Bah-*boom*. "Surprise."

"I *knew* you were my Secret Santa! I *knew* it!" Blade says. "You're such a good artist! The bunny card was amazing!"

Wow. I lean over and take a long, fake sip of water, and when I surface again, Blade is dangling the unwrapped shoelaces not like three scary snakes but like one perfect present.

"Siiiiiick," she says. Which sounds . . . wrong. But Blade goes, " 'Sick' is a compliment where I come from," and I go, "Oh, good!"

This seems like the right moment to run away.

But then Blade takes one of the black shoelaces and ties it around her wrist, which you'd think would be impossible to do by yourself—except, Blade is very coordinated. Athletic, practically.

"Ta-da," she says.

Just as she finishes triple-knotting the makeshift bracelet, I reach out and help her. "No, *here,*" she says, and Blade takes *my* wrist and ties the other shoelace around it. Everything that *isn't* my wrist itches and twitches and tingles and bah-*booms* at the same time. I have to force myself to talk.

"I didn't realize shoelaces could be bracelets," I say.

I feel like an empty mug that's being filled with hot chocolate. Like I've been getting warmer all week, and I finally found the hidden prize.

"Twins," Blade says, holding her wrist up to mine. They almost touch.

"Yeah," I say. "Something like that."

Blade nods, and a speck of dandruff falls from her head like a snowflake. I make a wish on it.

The bell goes off. It rings and rings even when it stops ringing.

Blade says, "Social studies," I say, "Band practice," and we make the same yuck face before heading in opposite directions.

But then she turns back around. "Hey, Sparkles—what's your real name?"

I catch sight of the hall monitor at the end of the corridor, five seconds away from giving us our first warning.

My lips go to say *Samantha,* but my mouth says, and just barely, "Flame."

Blade smiles. Her braces shine. "Flame. *Huh.* And they call *me* weird."

"This is your first warning, ladies," the hall monitor says.

We pivot from one another to head to our classes, but my Mary Janes turn me right around, *squeak.* "Blade?" I whisper.

"Yeah, Flame?"

"Second warning, ladies." Now the hall monitor is walking toward us.

"It's actually Sam," I blurt. "My name is Sam."

It's the first time I've corrected somebody in nearly a year. I brace myself to hear a joke about how Sam's a boy's name. To get teased. But Blade shimmies her wrist above her head, and the skull shoelace dances at the end of her arm. "Your secret's safe with me, Sam."

And right as the hall monitor arrives at my side, I say, "*Sick.*" And this time, I'm not whispering.

The Beans and Rice Chronicles of Isaiah Dunn

KELLY J. BAPTIST

December 31

"This gonna be one of them years," Mama says as we watch the ball drop on New Year's. She doesn't look at me when she says it, just stares at the TV.

"What you mean, Mama?" I ask. But she's holding tight to one of her bottles and takes a long swig instead of answering.

My stomach starts doing weird karate chops, but since my best friend, Sneaky, is here, I don't ask any more questions. When the fireworks start, me and Sneaky turn off the lamp, run to the window, and pull open the curtains to watch. The colors from the fireworks and the light from the TV dance around our dark living room. They make Mama's face look funny. When I glance at her, I see that her eyes are sad.

"Mama, should I wake Charlie up?" I ask.

Mama shakes her head. "Nah, let that baby sleep." She stops looking at the TV and stares at my sister, who's sucking on two fingers like a baby and cuddling up with her stuffed bunny. Mama gets up and puts a blanket on Charlie.

"You spending the night, Aaron?" she asks Sneaky. Mama's 'bout the only one who calls Sneaky by his real name. Even his own mama calls him Sneaky, and that's because when he was younger he was always sneaking something. Still does.

"Yeah, I think so," Sneaky says from the window. His mom is having an adults-only party in their apartment, so she sent him down here.

"Don't y'all be up too late," Mama says, taking her bottle with her. She always rips off the labels, but I know it's not pop.

Sneaky changes the channel to wrestling and we watch that for a while. When I go to the kitchen to get us a bag of chips, I hear Mama crying in her room and I know she's missing Daddy.

I take the chips back to the living room and turn the TV up so Sneaky won't know. Sneaky switches to a comedy channel, and I do my best to laugh whenever he does.

JANUARY 3

I wake up to Charlie poking me and pulling at my blanket, which is always annoying.

"'Saiah, Mama said for you to fix me something for breakfast."

"Huh?" I open one eye and Charlie's right up in my face. I push her away, but not too hard.

"Mama said for you to fix me something for breakfast." Charlie sticks her fingers in her mouth and waits for me to get up. She's four, and very smart, but she don't never listen when we tell her to stop sucking on her nasty fingers.

I crawl out the bed and yawn my way to the kitchen. Cereal's the easiest thing to make, but there's no milk. I open the freezer and grab some frozen waffles. I put four in the toaster and drink some orange juice straight from the carton.

"You ain't supposed to do that! I'm tellin' Mama!" Charlie says, making a face.

"You tell her and you ain't gettin' no waffles." I wipe my mouth with the back of my hand and take another sip. "And I'll tell her you're sucking your fingers."

Charlie pulls them out her mouth, wipes the slime on her pajama pants, and sighs. The waffles pop up and I put them on a plate and butter them. I put one on Charlie's Dora the Explorer plate and look for the syrup. There's barely any left, and Charlie laughs when the bottle makes fart sounds.

"Say your grace," I tell her.

"Jesus, bless my waffle, and help us get more syrup. Amen." Charlie stares at the waffle. "You suppose to cut it like Mama does, 'Saiah."

I sigh and cut her waffle real quick. Then I put two waffles on a plate, squeeze some farting syrup onto them, and walk to Mama's room. Her door's open a crack, and I knock and peek inside before I open it.

"Mama, you hungry? Cuz I made waffles."

Mama's bundled up in her bed like I was before Charlie woke me. She doesn't move a bit, even when I sit next to her.

"You make Charlie something?" Mama's voice is muffled and scratchy from under the covers.

"Yeah, she's eating."

"All right. Y'all eat and watch TV, okay? I'll be up in a little while."

"So you don't want the waffles?" I ask, staring at the plate.

"No, just go watch your sister and let Mama rest. Get dressed for school."

I don't tell Mama it's Sunday, so there's no school. I cut a bite of the waffles with the fork and chew it. A few of Mama's bottles are on the floor. Empty. Then I notice a gold notebook peeking out from under the bed. It looks like one of the notebooks Daddy would always take with him to work, so I quickly reach down and grab it.

"Go, Isaiah!" Mama says, and it sounds like a groan. I scurry back to the kitchen and slide into a chair across from Charlie.

"Why you eating Mama's food?" Charlie asks.

"She didn't want it," I say with my mouth full. Charlie makes a face.

"Probably because you didn't cut them right," she says, picking at her waffles.

"If you don't want them, you can get up and be hungry," I say, tired of her being so picky. Charlie doesn't say anything else, but she hums while she eats the rest of her food. I get the last waffle from the toaster and eat it without syrup.

"Can I have a banana?" Charlie asks, looking at the bowl on the table. There are two bananas, and they both look pretty bad to me, but I shrug and tell her okay. She eats her mushy banana and asks for water, "Cuz you slobbed on the orange juice, 'Saiah." I pour her the water, then we go sit on the couch and watch cartoons.

Mama stays in her room all day.

JANUARY 5

There are papers taped to the door when I get home from school. I pull them off and hand them to Mama when I go inside. She's lying on the couch, watching some talk show. She looks at the papers and doesn't say anything, just sets them aside. The good thing is, there are no bottles around her.

"Where's Charlie?" I ask, dropping my backpack onto a chair.

"Miz Rita's doing her hair," Mama says. "She's probably done by now." She shifts a little and points to the chair. "Hand me my purse, 'Saiah."

Mama pulls out a twenty-dollar bill and hands it to me. "Go get your sister and tell Miz Rita I said thanks."

I push the money in my pocket and take the stairs down to the first floor, where Miz Rita lives. Her daughter, Shayna, opens the door.

"Hey, Isaiah. You comin' for Charlie?"

"Yeah," I say, stepping into the apartment. It's warm and cozy inside, and unlike our place, I smell food cooking.

"They're in the kitchen. Mama's almost done." Shayna's watching TV and doing homework at the same time, which never works for me.

Charlie comes bouncing into the room, and she's got tiny, neat cornrows with tons of beads at the ends.

"You like it?" she asks me, shaking her head from side to side so the beads make lots of noise.

"Yeah, it's nice," I say. Miz Rita comes in and I stand and hand her the money.

"Mama said to tell you thank you."

"Uh-uh, you tell your mama not to worry about it." Miz Rita shakes her head at my hand holding the money.

"She said to give this to you—"

"And I'm telling you to give it right back to her," Miz Rita says. "And make sure she gets it, Isaiah. Don't be buying candy or something with it."

"I'll give it to her," I promise, putting the money into my pocket. "C'mon, Charlie. Say thank you to Miz Rita."

"Thank you, Miz Rita!" Charlie says, giving her a big hug. "Can I have some of what you have for dinner?"

"Charlie!" I say, cuz I know Mama wouldn't want her asking for anything. Inside, though, I'm wanting some of Miz Rita's food, too.

Miz Rita just laughs. "You want a plate of food, baby? Isaiah, you think your mama will mind?"

"Um, no. I don't think so." I lie.

"Well, y'all come on to the kitchen."

I follow Miz Rita and sit at her table while she fixes us some chicken, rice and gravy, corn bread, and string beans. It smells so good, I have to close my mouth real tight so I don't drool. When she sets the plate in front of me, I'm already into my first bite when Charlie starts to say grace.

"Thank you, Miz Rita, it's really good," I manage to say around swallows.

"You're welcome, baby." Miz Rita gets another plate. "And I'ma fix a plate for your mama, too, okay?"

This time, my mouth is full, so I just nod.

Miz Rita asks if we want seconds, but I say no. I can't turn down Miz Rita's pound cake and butter pecan ice cream, though. I let the sweet ice cream stay in my mouth as long as I can, then crunch up the pecans. The ice cream reminds me of Daddy. Butter pecan was his favorite.

We thank Miz Rita again and take the plate of food for Mama. On the elevator, Charlie swings her head and clacks her beads all the way to the seventh floor.

"This is way better than how Mama did my hair, right, 'Saiah?" she asks.

I think about the giant afro puff that Charlie had been wearing for almost a month.

"Yeah, it is," I agree.

The apartment's dark when we go inside. I turn on the lamp and peek inside Mama's room. She's in bed again.

"Mama? Miz Rita sent a plate of food for you," I say quietly.

"Mmmmmm" is all Mama says.

"I'll put it on the counter."

Mama doesn't answer, so I just go out and close her door. I help Charlie take a bath and tuck her into bed. She's so sleepy, she don't even fuss. Then I turn on the TV in the living room, real low, and wait for Mama to come eat.

I fall asleep on the couch and wake up at 2:17 a.m. When I check the kitchen, the plate's still on the counter. I put it in the fridge, turn off the TV and the lights, and get into bed thinking that if Daddy had known things would be like this, he probably wouldn't have died.

JANUARY 10

I wish me and Sneaky were in the same class, like last year. We had mad fun in Ms. Clancy's class, and she always let us work together. This year, Sneaky has Mr. Pollard, who's real tall and kinda looks like Kevin Garnett. I'm stuck with Mrs. Fisher, who gives the most homework of all the fifth-grade teachers.

Even after school, I don't get to hang with Sneaky. Mama told me to walk to the library instead of catching the bus and that she would pick me up at five. The library is quiet inside and has the same book smell that the one at school has. The computers are all taken, so I sit at a table by a window and start my homework.

I decide that social studies can wait when I spot the gold notebook hidden behind my Pistons hoodie. I don't know why, but my heart is beating fast, and my stomach is karate-chopping when I hold the notebook. Daddy would always say, "It's not quite ready yet," when I'd ask what he was writing. Now it's like he's sitting here with me, grinning and excited for me to finally read what's inside. I open the notebook and see *The Beans and Rice Chronicles of Isaiah Dunn* written in my dad's handwriting.

"Whoa!" I whisper. Daddy must've been writing about me! I start reading. In the stories, Isaiah Dunn is a kid who gets superpowers whenever he eats his mother's rice and beans. He travels around the world to help kids in danger, and the president always calls on him for secret missions.

I forget about the time and keep reading until a guy taps me on the shoulder.

"We're closing in fifteen minutes," he says.

"Okay," I say. I keep reading until I get to the bottom of the page, then I close the notebook and put it into my backpack. It's dark outside and I know it's way past five o'clock.

I wander around the library looking for Mama until they flicker the lights and announce that the library is closing. I wait outside in the freezing cold for what feels like forever before I see Mama's car pull up. I race over, excited to tell her about Daddy's stories.

But I forget all that when I see that the car is stuffed with all our things.

FEBRUARY 7

"You smell like you been smoking." Angel Atkins leans toward me and sniffs. She wrinkles her nose, which makes her look even uglier than normal.

"Maybe I have," I tell her. Mama, Charlie, and I have been in room number 109 at the Sleep Inn for three weeks, and it still smells like cigarette smoke.

"Well, you can't kiss Gabi on Valentine's Day if you got smoke breath," she says with a smirk. I wish Angel and I didn't sit at the same table. I wish Sneaky were here instead of Angel, who is *nothing* like her name.

"I ain't kissin' nobody!" I say, glaring at Angel.

"Mr. Dunn, Miss Atkins. Is there something more interesting than the reading assignment? Something you want to share with everyone?"

"No," Angel says, rolling her eyes. I don't say anything.

"Mr. Dunn? Is there a reason you can't focus on your work?"

"I'm focusing on my work," I say, and I start reading the stupid worksheet she gave us and answer the questions at the end. Daddy's stories are way more interesting than this.

After lunch, Angel passes me a note. It's a really bad picture of me holding a cigarette and Gabriella running away. I ball up the paper and throw it right at Angel's big head.

"Isaiah Dunn!" Mrs. Fisher jumps from her desk and is in my face in a second. "What has gotten into you? We do not throw things at other students!"

"She was messin' with *me*, Mrs. Fisher," I try to explain. "And it was just a piece of paper."

"Isaiah, you apologize now, or you go to the principal's office. Do you understand?"

Maybe because it's Friday, or maybe because Angel's grinning like she's so smart. Maybe it's just because it smells like something died in Mrs. Fisher's mouth, but the next thing I know, I'm sayin', "Yeah, I understand that you don't need to be all in my face with your breath smellin' like that!"

Mrs. Fisher's mouth drops open, and so does Angel's. The class is dead quiet, until a few kids start laughing. I glare at Mrs. Fisher and she points to the door.

"Go to Mr. Tobin's office! Now!"

I leave the classroom and walk down the quiet hall to the principal's office. Inside, Mr. Tobin lectures me about respect and kindness before giving me detention, which I don't mind because it means less time at Smoky Inn. But my day gets even worse, because as soon as I climb into the car, Mama lets me have it.

"You betta cut out all this foolishness, Isaiah," she says. "I've been waiting a whole hour for you!"

"Sorry," I mumble, buckling my seat belt. I don't say anything about *me* having to wait at the library, or my clothes always smelling like smoke. The way I see it, Mama's kinda the reason I had detention in the first place.

FEBRUARY 10

"I'm always interrupting your reading, aren't I?"

"Huh?" I look up from Daddy's notebook and see the library guy heading over to my table.

"You like to read?" the guy asks. I know he works here, but he doesn't seem like a librarian to me.

"Sometimes," I say.

"Sometimes is better than no times," the guy says. He holds out his hand for a fist bump. "We haven't officially met. I'm Mr. Shephard, youth services librarian. What's your name?"

"Isaiah," I say.

"Cool." Mr. Shephard glances at the notebook. "So you're a writer?"

"Not really," I say. "But my dad is."

"Oh yeah? Well, you'll have to tell him about our short story contest. Hold on a second and I'll get you more information."

Mr. Shephard heads over to his desk before I can tell him that my dad only *used* to write. When he comes back, he hands me a green flyer.

"The literacy council holds a writing contest every February. The deadline's in two weeks."

"Thanks," I say, taking the paper.

My eyes get big when I read that the grand prize is $300! Daddy's stories are way better than *Blue Harbor,* the book we're reading in school. I bet he could win the contest!

Even after they flicker the lights and announce that the library is closing, I just keep reading how to enter over and over again.

An idea starts forming in my mind, and I wonder which story Daddy would enter if he were here. One thing's for sure, I don't have a lot of time to figure it out.

It's Valentine's Day. Mama makes pancakes using what she calls a hot plate. The pancakes are supposed to be heart-shaped, but they look like circles with little dents. We don't even have farting syrup this time, so we have to eat them plain.

"Isaiah, I want you to wash the dishes and sweep up," Mama says after breakfast. She climbs back into bed and closes her eyes. "Then maybe you can take Charlie outside for a little while so I can rest."

"It's freezing out there, Mama," I say.

"Just for a little while, 'Saiah!" she says.

I wash the dishes and put them on a towel to dry. Then I grab the broom and sweep up the crumbs that Charlie's spilled on the floor. Mama's under the covers now, and I wonder if she's asleep. So much for asking her to take me to the library.

Charlie's coloring Disney Princesses and looks just fine, so I plop down on the couch and turn the TV on low. I pass all the kiddie channels quick so Charlie won't start whining about watching one of them. I stop when I get to a kung fu movie with Bruce Lee. Mama and Charlie would always make faces and go watch something on the other TV when me and Daddy watched kung fu movies. I look at Charlie, and yup, she's making a face, even though she's still coloring.

When the movie's over, Charlie asks to hang her pictures on the wall. I find some tape and we put Jasmine and Sleeping Beauty and Cinderella all over the room. I'm not into princess stuff, of course, but I think the pictures make the room look way better.

"I'm hungry," Charlie says after we tape up the pictures. I warm up some beans and rice for her in the little microwave, wishing that it could give me superpowers like in Daddy's stories.

"You're not hungry?" Charlie asks me when I don't sit at the table with her.

"Nah, I'm tired of beans and rice," I say.

"Me too," says Charlie, but she eats up the whole bowl.

FEBRUARY 23

"Can we go to the library, Mama?"

"Not now, Isaiah," Mama says.

I suck my teeth, because the deadline for the story contest is tomorrow, and I have to finish typing Daddy's story. I decided to use the one where Isaiah Dunn saves his mom from a sinking cruise ship. I've been working on it every day after school, and Sneaky thinks I'm crazy for carrying an extra notebook around and always wanting to be at the library. All I know is that it beats being crammed in the motel room, where there's nothing to do but trip over each other and watch the same reruns on TV. Plus, Charlie's always making noise and nobody tells her to shut up but me.

Mama makes beans and rice for dinner *again,* but I pour myself a bowl of cereal instead.

"You too good to have what we're having?" Mama asks while I crunch on my flakes.

"No," I say. "Just tired of always eating beans and rice."

"Tired of the food we got?" Mama shakes her head, makes it seem like she's not tired of eating the same thing, too. I don't answer, but I feel my stomach start jumping around.

"Shoot, when you get a job and start buying the groceries, then you can decide what you're tired of eating!" Mama says.

"When are *you* gonna get a job, Mama?"

Mama stares at me and I stare back. I can't believe I said that to her, even if I been thinking it for a while. She gets up and before I can move, I feel the sting of her hand against my cheek.

"You grown enough to question me about what I do? You think your daddy would want you talking like that?" She's mad, and her eyes are flashing. Well, I'm mad, too!

"You're not the only one who misses him!" I yell. "And he wouldn't want us living in this stupid motel with no money cuz you use it to get drunk!"

Charlie's mouth falls open, but Mama just stands there

frozen. I grab my backpack and coat, storm out the room, and slam the door.

It's dark outside and cold enough to make my eyes water, but I take off running and don't stop until my lungs feel like they're gonna explode and I get a cramp in my side. I slow down and walk the rest of the way to the library.

It's warm inside, and I hurry to find an empty computer. My fingers fly across the keyboard as I finish typing Daddy's story. I spell-check everything just as they start to flicker the lights.

"Just five more minutes," I plead with Mr. Shephard. He turns out to be a pretty cool dude, and gives me just enough time to e-mail the story.

I give a sigh of relief and lean back in the chair, feeling good. Someone taps me on the shoulder, and I turn around, expecting Mr. Shephard.

It's Mama. Charlie's with her, sucking on her nasty fingers.

"Thought you'd be here." She doesn't smile, but she doesn't sound angry anymore, either.

"How'd you know?" I ask.

"I just had a feeling," Mama says. "Your daddy would always come here, too. It was one of his favorite places."

I pick up the notebook and show Mama.

"Did you know Daddy was writing stories about me? Did he show you?"

Mama smiles as she flips through the pages.

"I forgot all about this one," she says. "He started writing in it after you were born, but I never knew what it actually was."

I tell her about the contest and how I entered Daddy's story and her eyes get happy and sad at the same time.

"Oh, Isaiah," she says, "he would be so proud."

Mr. Shephard comes over again and says hello to Mama.

"It's hard to pull him out of here, isn't it?" Mr. Shephard says with a warm smile.

"Yes, it is." Mama puts her arm around me. "He's just like his father."

"Well, he's always reading when I see him, and trust me, librarians love that!" Mr. Shephard turns to me. "What book are you reading now?"

I don't even hesitate.

"The Beans and Rice Chronicles of Isaiah Dunn," I say.

"Hmm, haven't heard of that one," he says.

I smile.

"Not yet."

Choctaw Bigfoot, Midnight in the Mountains

TIM TINGLE

Blame my uncle Kenneth. Everybody else does.

Saturday afternoon, sitting under the trees in the backyard of Mawmaw, my Choctaw grandmother. The family was gathered for our weekly Saturday meal, *dozens of cousins* and aunts and uncles and everybody kin to us. Barbeque cooked on the grill, beef and chicken and fat sausage links, my favorite.

"You know better than to listen to anything that man says," said my mother, sliding the glass patio door open and hollering loud enough for everybody to hear.

My little cousin Cindy had just run in the house screaming about some swamp creature from Mississippi.

"But Uncle Kenneth said . . ."

"I don't care what your uncle Kenneth says, now or twenty years from now."

Uncle Kenneth sat on a chair by the fishpond, with his head resting on his chest. He was pretending to be asleep, but nobody bought it. As soon as Mom stepped inside to check on her pot of beans, Kenneth smiled and waved a finger at me. The other grown-ups looked at each other and shook their heads.

That's when you know, really know, you're surrounded by family. Nobody has to say a word. They just look at each other and you know what they are thinking.

I sauntered across the yard like I was searching for fallen pecans on the ground. When I reached Uncle Kenneth, I sat down by his chair and wrapped my arms around my knees.

"You know your mother is a smart lady," Uncle Kenneth said.

I looked up at him and waited. He didn't say anything, but the way he looked to the house and back at me told me, *but she doesn't know everything*. He didn't say it, he *Choctaw-said* it. We're Choctaws and we have our own ways, trust me.

I laughed and nodded a Choctaw *yes*.

"So, I already told you about the Bohpoli, those Choctaw little people," Uncle Kenneth said. "And you know not to trust them. They aren't gonna go hurt anybody, no broken arms or sliced-off fingers—that's not what they're about."

"They're funny, aren't they, Uncle Kenneth?"

"That's right, Turtle Kid," he said. "The Bohpoli like to

play jokes. And they can be invisible when they want to, so they're really good at joke-playing. Uh, you don't mind me calling you Turtle Kid, do you?"

"No, I like that name."

"Good, that'll be your Choctaw name for now. So anyway, the Bohpoli were following a family down the road. They might have been driving a wagon pulled by horses or maybe a car, I can't remember."

"I think it was a car, 'cause it happened last year," I said. "And it was in those Oklahoma Kiamichi Mountains and it was almost midnight."

"You know this story?"

"No, uh, sorry," I said, zipping my fingers across my mouth, the Choctaw sign for *I'll shut up*.

"*Hoke,* then. But it *was* last year, it *was* the Kiamichi Mountains, and it *was* near midnight, so the night creatures were prowling. The driver, Mr. Chukma, pulled to the side of the road. He spotted a clearing under the trees and thought it would be a good place to spend the night. He stepped from the car, getting ready to open the door for his wife and wake up his three kids. That's when he heard it."

I wanted so bad to ask, *Heard what?* But I'd already zipped my mouth shut. Instead, I leaned forward.

"Yes," Uncle Kenneth whispered, looking about the yard and making sure nobody else heard what he was about to say. "That's when he heard it."

I nodded. Slowly.

"POW!" he hollered, slapping his hands together.

I fell over backward, and everybody within a mile laughed so loud my mother stuck her head through the back door again.

"Don't say I didn't warn you," she said. More laughter.

"Pay no attention to them, Turtle Kid," said my dear uncle. "I want this to be a story you'll never forget."

I sat up and said quietly, "You don't have to worry about that."

"Achukma, good. Now where was I? Oh, so Mr. Chukma heard the *POW* noise and jumped back in the car. He pulled his wife close to him and told the kids to get down on the floorboard and stay quiet. They didn't have long to wait. Mr. Chukma was leaning over the seat and assuring his kids that everything was gonna be all right, so he had his back turned to the front windshield.

"Mrs. Chukma tapped him softly on the shoulder and whispered, 'You need to look.' Mr. Chukma was about to ask, *What is it?* but he didn't get a chance. He heard a growl so loud the kids screamed and Mrs. Chukma screamed and finally Mr. Chukma himself screamed.

"Naloosha Chitto, the big hairy man of Choctaw country, stood right in front of the car."

"Oh no."

"That's right, Turtle Kid, the Big Hairy Man, Naloosha

Chitto. That's what we Choctaws call him. He circled the car, waving a log so big no human could have carried it. But he swung it back and forth, from his shoulder to his palm, slapping it like it was a foot-long ruler, like you have in school."

By now *dozens of cousins* had scooted around me, sprawled about on the ground and listening. Uncle Kenneth took a long, deep breath, and when he leaned forward again, the world changed. No longer were we in the backyard of Pasadena, Texas, the Goode backyard of my Choctaw grandmother. No, we were in the dark, deep woods of the Oklahoma Kiamichi Mountains, clinging to each other and praying that the Choctaw Bigfoot, the Naloosha Chitto, would please go away.

"Now, I'm not gonna tell you he smashed the hood of that car so hard he cracked the engine block and they couldn't drive away. But that's what happened. And when he finished with the hood, he flung the log at the windshield and glass went scattering everywhere."

"Oh no!" shouted *dozens of cousins*.

"Now, I'm not gonna tell you Mr. Chukma and his family lost fingers and eyeballs and noses and ears, with all that glass flying about. 'Cause that's not what happened. No, they had old Choctaw blankets wrapped around 'em, so they were safe.

"Well, not entirely safe. Mr. Chukma flung open his door

and Mrs. Chukma dragged the three kids out of the car, and just in time.

"Naloosha Chitto jumped on the smashed hood and pounded the roof of the car with his log. The Chukmas fled to the woods and hid behind a big boulder. They wrapped one big blanket over themselves and shook and shivered under it."

"Naloosha Chitto climbed from the car and looked for the Chukmas, didn't he?" I asked. I was lying on the ground now, with my face buried in the green grass. I whispered so softly not a single blade of grass moved.

"Yes, he did," said Uncle Kenneth. "He ran across the road and struck everything in his way. He knocked down a tree where a mountain lion slept, but even the mountain lion didn't want to fight Naloosha Chitto, not at midnight, so he leapt to the ground and ran away. Then everything grew quiet. Real quiet. Strange and quiet, like you never know, living in the city.

"Nothing moved. No birds, not even crickets chirping. Nothing. Naloosha Chitto had scared every living thing in those woods, and he liked it. He knew that when the Chukmas moved, even a tiny little step, he'd hear 'em. So he sat down, pulled out a corncob, and ate a few bites."

Uncle Kenneth turned to me and asked, "I bet you thought I forgot all about those Bohpoli?" I shook my head no, then lowered my chin to my chest and waited. Like the Chukmas, we all waited.

"Yes, those Bohpoli, the Choctaw little people, they always seem to show up when they're least expected. And who's gonna be looking for the funny Bohpoli when Naloosha Chitto is smashing cars and trees and everything in sight? But anyways, they floated above the tree he leaned against."

"Floated?" I whisper-asked.

"Oh yes, Turtle Kid. They can appear and disappear and time-travel and do anything they want to, those Bohpoli. They floated above him and started making chirping noises, like little birdies. And, oh, did that make Naloosha Chitto mad! He threw his corncob at the birdies, but they kept on chirping.

"So he climbed the tree, dragging his log behind him. Halfway up the tree, thirty feet high—the chirping stopped. He grunted a few times and looked up and down and all around. The Bohpoli started chirping again, on the end of the limb.

"Now, Naloosha Chitto, I don't care what they tell you, is not no idiot. No, he isn't. He knew not to climb out on that limb, heavy as he was. But he did scoot a few feet away from the trunk. And he did stretch his log out to the end of the limb. Then he stood up, careful not to lose his balance and fall, and slowly lifted the log over his head, ready to smash those chirpy birdies.

"That's when they did it, the Bohpoli. They started chirping louder than ever, from the other end of the limb, the trunk side. And Naloosha Chitto was *soooo* mad, he turned around and smashed the limb he was standing on!

"Now, I'm not gonna tell you he fell forty feet to the ground and knocked himself out, and the Chukmas heard it all and slept peacefully till morning, when they hitched a ride to town and lived happily ever after."

"Because that's not what happened, is it, Uncle Kenneth?" I asked.

"No, Turtle Kid. It's never that simple, not when the Bohpoli are involved."

"What happened?"

"Remember I said the Chukmas covered themselves with a Choctaw blanket? Well, Mrs. Chukma always carried a few spare blankets in the trunk of the car. And with the car smashed to smithereens, the trunk flew open. The Bohpoli spotted the extra blankets, and while one Bohpoli was chirping like a bird, the others hurried across the road and grabbed a beautiful blue Choctaw blanket. They flew to the base of the tree and stretched it wide like a trampoline."

We all, myself and my *dozens of cousins,* leaned back and raised our eyebrows in disbelief. *Like,* hoke, *never gonna happen. Naloosha Chitto had to weigh at least a thousand pounds, and a few little people could never catch him and bounce him around like a kid on a trampoline.*

"I know what you're thinking," Uncle Kenneth said. "You're thinking, *How could they cross the road without a crossing guard?*"

We all gave him a great big authentic Choctaw laugh and let him go on with his story.

"So when Naloosha Chitto cracked the limb he was standing on and fell seventy-seven feet to the ground, he spun round and round, brushing away the clouds and swiping at the moon. But nothing stopped his fall.

"He hit the blanket like a boulder from the sky, as four strong-willed Bohpoli yanked hard at the four corners. Luckily, Mrs. Chukma had a mighty fine recipe for Naloosha Chitto stew in her cookbook.

"Unluckily, she'd left the cookbook in their kitchen drawer in McAlester.

"Luckily, she'd memorized the recipe for just this occasion.

"Unlucky for the Chukma family, but lucky for Naloosha Chitto, he did not end up in a stew pot.

"No. He bounced high in the air, once, twice, four times, before settling on the ground, sitting Indian-style and very relieved."

"Uncle Kenneth?"

"Yes, Turtle Kid?"

"What is Indian-style?"

"Glad you asked. Indian-style means in a chair, like you sit in at school. The Bohpoli found a flimsy folding chair in the car trunk and had it ready for Naloosha Chitto."

"*Hoke,* just wondering."

"And once he realized he wasn't going to die, Naloosha

Chitto was madder than he'd ever been in his life. He jumped out of the chair and flung it so high, it sailed over the Red River and all the way to Love Field Airport in Dallas. It came so close to hitting the wing of a plane, it was mistaken for a drone.

"The Chukmas watched everything, peeking over the boulder and hoping Naloosha Chitto would live but maybe be knocked out for a few days. When he stood up, Mr. Chukma hollered, 'Balili! Run!' And that's what they did, downhill to the state park.

"Naloosha Chitto heard the shouting and chased the Chukmas. He ran across the road—first looking to his right, then to his left—to make sure no cars were coming.

"Paths cut through the trees and made it easier to run, even on a dark midnight. Of course, the path was covered with sleeping rattlesnakes, a family of porcupines, and mountains of scorpions, but nothing serious. But this was a park the Chukmas did not know. They'd never camped here. They only knew they had to make it to park headquarters before Naloosha Chitto caught 'em.

"Mr. Chukma ran in the lead, slapping branches out of the way, lifting and tossing fallen trees stretched across the path. Mrs. Chukma hurried the kids along, trying her best to keep the blanket over their heads. She was scared to blazes, but she acted brave for the kids.

"All of a sudden the path split. One fork curved to the

left, the other to the right. And right in the middle of the fork stood a tall sign with big letters and an arrow. On any day but today, or tonight, the sign read DOWNHILL TO LAKESIDE PICNIC GROUNDS, LEFT and the arrow at the top of the sign pointed left.

"But not tonight. You see, those Bohpoli were having too much fun to quit. So they switched the arrows, pointing 'em in the wrong direction. Tonight the sign read DOWNHILL TO LAKESIDE PICNIC GROUNDS, LEFT but the arrow pointed right.

"So the Chukmas ran faster to the left. When they came to the next fork, the sign read DOWNHILL TO LAKESIDE BOAT DOCK, RIGHT but the arrow at the top of the sign pointed left.

"Ignoring the arrow, they ran downhill to the right. Finally, after dodging rattlesnakes and scorpions, they spotted the sign they were looking for: PARK RANGER HEADQUARTERS, DOWNHILL RIGHT but the arrow at the top of the sign pointed left.

"The Chukma family turned right and ran like their lives depended on it. They skidded and rolled and didn't stop till they came to the bottom of the hill. But they weren't safe yet. They still had to cross the picnic grounds and parking lot, and they knew how fast Naloosha Chitto could run."

"He was right behind 'em," I said.

"No, Turtle Kid, he was two miles away, running in the wrong direction."

"I'm confused," said Trisha, my younger cousin.

"Like, duh," said Keith, the smartest cousin.

I just sat back without saying a word, folding my arms and Choctaw-saying with my pursed lips and tilting head, Hoke, *so where is this going?*

Uncle Kenneth pretended not to notice me, but I saw a smile creeping over his face.

"But if the Chukmas were gonna make it alive and not into the belly of Naloosha Chitto, they had to make sense out of this confusion. The Big Dude was fast and getting close. But he couldn't read, and when a sign pointed right or left, he followed the arrow. Didn't matter what the *sign* said, he followed the arrow."

"How did the Chukmas know which way to go," I asked, "if the arrow pointed the wrong way?"

"Glad you asked," said Uncle Kenneth. "I didn't tell you about the Chukma kids yet. They were smart young 'uns, real smart. Mary Chukma was twelve years old and she loved geography. Whenever they traveled, she always carried a state map. And did it come in handy on this night!"

"How could she read in the dark?" Keith asked.

"Thank you for asking," Uncle Kenneth said. "Ricky Chukma, Mary's little brother, had a camper's manual which he had read from cover to cover. It advised what to carry in case a Naloosha Chitto smashed your car and you were stranded in the woods at midnight. He remembered chapter two, 'The Importance of Flashlights in the Dark,' so of course he carried a flashlight.

"With Ricky shining the light and Mary reading the map, the Chukmas knew which way to go. They dashed across the parking lot to the park headquarters, pounded on the door, and a park ranger ushered them inside to safety."

"What happened to their car?" Keith asked. "I am assuming it was totaled?"

"You assume right," said Uncle Kenneth. "But the rearview mirrors were still good, so AllChoctaw State Insurance replaced the Chukma car with a super cool minivan!"

I couldn't let him get away with that. I covered my eyes with my hands and shook my head, Choctaw-telling him, *My mom is right, you can't believe a word Uncle Kenneth says*.

"Excuse me, Uncle Kenneth," said Keith, and the academic tone of his voice made everyone pause and look his way.

"Yes, my nephew Keith, son of my brother Billy," said Uncle Kenneth. *Sarcasm*, I whispered in my fists, rocking back and forth.

"I am pondering the fate of campers who arrived the next day," said Keith. "Nice families who could not read, or possibly read in another language?"

"You're forgetting," Uncle Kenneth replied, "those Bohpoli think of everything. They of course switched back the arrows. So, if there are no more questions . . ."

"But what happened to Naloosha Chitto?" asked sweet little cousin Cindy, waving her tiny hand in the air. "He is people, too."

"Glad you asked," Uncle Kenneth said, glancing at his watch and blowing his cheeks into one huge *I am not believing this* Choctaw bubble. "Yes, Naloosha Chitto is people, too. But he found himself running uphill till he came to the twenty-foot-long boulder stretched over the lake, ninety-seven feet below. The sign clearly said: DO NOT WALK ON THE OVERLOOK. IT IS CRACKED AND READY TO FALL AND WE DO NOT HAVE THE STAFF TO PROVIDE A LIFEGUARD IF YOU CANNOT SWIM. OR EVEN IF YOU CAN."

"But Naloosha Chitto can't read, Uncle Kenneth," Cindy chirped.

"No, sweetheart, he cannot. He ignored the warning and stepped onto the overlook. He heard the *CURRRrrRACKing* sound, lost his balance, and fell kicking and screaming into the lake."

"Kicking and screaming?" asked Trisha.

"It's called a cliché," replied Keith.

"I don't like this!" said a determined little Cindy.

"Wait, hon, it's not over yet," said Uncle Kenneth. "A group of anthropologists, seeking proof that Naloosha Chitto was real, were paddling their canoe around the lake. When they saw not only the skeletal structure of the creature, but the actual *creature,* they leapt overboard. Naloosha Chitto climbed in the canoe and paddled safely to shore."

"Why were they paddling around at midnight?" Keith asked.

"And did they live or drown?" asked Trisha.

"Yeah, Uncle Kenneth, and what kind of creamer did the park ranger serve the Chukmas in their coffee?" I inquired.

Uncle Kenneth stood up, looming six feet above me and my *dozens of cousins*. He took a deep breath and bellowed, "*The END!*"

Like good little Choctaw kids, me and my *dozens of cousins* all clapped and slapped Uncle Kenneth on the back. "Good story!" we told him.

"Wait," he said, holding his palm aloft. "What could the Chukmas do that Naloosha Chitto could not do? What saved this family's life?"

"Turtle Kid knows," I said, raising my hand.

"Yes?"

I stood up and lifted my palm to Uncle Kenneth, in a sign of high respect, then turned to my *dozens of cousins*. "Our dear and wise Uncle Kenneth has told us a tale full of meaning. The Chukma family can do many things Naloosha Chitto cannot, but the greatest of these, my *dozens of cousins,* the greatest of these things is that they can—each and every one of them—tie their own shoelaces."

Jaws dropped and no one said a word.

"If they couldn't tie their shoelaces they would have tripped on the path, and who knows what would have happened?"

"Is there anything else they could do that Naloosha Chitto could not?" asked Uncle Kenneth. "Anything?"

"Well, *hoke*. They could read. Mary Chukma could read

and so could her brother Ricky. They could read in the dark with flashlights. They could read even while they ate hamburgers."

"And French fries!" shouted Cindy. "With lots of ketchup!"

"But they were always careful never to drip ketchup on the pages of the book," Keith said. "Nobody wants to read a book with ketchup between the pages."

"I told you never to listen to your uncle Kenneth!" my mother shouted, standing in the doorway with her hands on her hips. "Is he telling you to pour ketchup on your books?"

"*No!*" we all shouted, protecting our new and funniest favorite teacher, Uncle Kenneth. Mother closed the door and stepped inside, and I thought—for just a moment—that I saw her smiling.

"*Hoke*, Uncle Kenneth," I asked, "how do you know so much about Naloosha Chitto?"

"Naloosha Chitto, the Choctaw Trail of Tears, the Choctaw Code Talkers of World War One, I know all about Choctaws, today and long ago. And other Indian nations, too. Anybody want to guess how?"

"Turtle Kid knows," I said.

"I'm sure you do," said Uncle Kenneth. "I'm sure you do."

"You know all about Choctaws because my mother read to you when you were a little kid."

Uncle Kenneth gave me a quiet *Are you crazy?* Choctaw stare, then his lips crawled into a grin. "Or maybe," he said, "I learned to read before I learned to tie my own shoelaces!"

"No way!" shouted my *dozens of cousins,* and we circled my Uncle Kenneth for one big Choctaw hug.

Main Street

JACQUELINE WOODSON

Autumn now. The leaves here in New Hampshire are the ones on postcards—bright red and heartbreaking gold, color so deep and intense it seems it doesn't belong in nature. They sell the postcards at the pharmacy on Main Street and tourists buy tons of them, scribbling things like *Gorgeous here* and *Right out of Our Town* and *Bringing you home some maple syrup* and *I can imagine living here one day*. Celeste said that's how her mother found Peterborough. She had come up with a busload of people wanting to see the leaves turn colors. And she said to herself, *Maybe one day I'll live here*. Celeste said, *Maybe she was so busy looking at the colored leaves, she didn't look around to see that the leaves were the ONLY color in this town!*

There's a coffee shop on Main—right next to the pharmacy. Even though egg creams weren't always on the menu, the people coming here to look at the leaves kept asking for them so the owner finally added them and people coming from the city drink them by the gallon and write their postcards. I haven't learned to like the egg creams, but I sit at the coffee shop some days, drinking Cokes and looking over people's shoulders to watch them write the same things— over and over and over. Sometimes I think I'll see Celeste getting out of a car and running into the drugstore with her mother. But Celeste is gone now. This town is both completely different—and absolutely the same—without her.

Last winter the snow fell so long and rose so high, my father hired a man from Keene to plow it. When the man arrived, his huge plow moved silently through the mass of snow. The silence surprised me. How could so much power exist inside such quiet? As I watched, pressing my head against the window, I said to my father, *I want to move through the world that quietly. That powerfully.*

Where did you come from? my father said, his eyes at once laughing and worried.

I had a mother once, I said into the pane. *She used to say things.*

Don't say that, my father said. *You still do. Don't ever say that.*

But he is wrong. I don't have a mother anymore. It's just my father now. And the leaves. And the snow.

And the memory.

There are things you're not allowed to say. When I was very young, it was the curses I'd heard my mother use, the words erupting from her mouth but disconnected—too ugly to belong to someone as beautiful as my mother. One morning, I stood in front of the mirror, saying the words over and over. My father found me this way. Neither of us knew that exactly eight days from that moment, my mother would move on to the next place. We thought the doctors were wrong. We prayed, *Please, doctors, in the name of our Holy Father, be wrong.*

What are you saying? my father said when he heard me. *Don't ever say those words. Ever.*

But Mama says them.

She's in pain, my father said. *Those words should only be said by people in pain.*

I wanted to tell him I *was* in pain. I wanted to show him where it hurt. Point to my head, my heart, my belly. Say, *Here, Daddy. And here. And here.* But I didn't. I was eight years old. He would say I was too young to know real pain. *After all,* he'd say, *you've never even had a skinned knee, Treetop!* Then rub my head and smile that halfway real, halfway crying smile. That winter, I hurt every place my mother hurt. As I pressed wet cloths to her sweating forehead, as I let her hold my hand to wait out the pain, as I read to her from gossip magazines and gently brushed her thinning hair, each twist of pain moving through her moved through me. I wanted to tell my father this—that once I had lived inside my mother, a part of her. I wanted to say, *How could I NOT know her pain?*

❈

What kind of name is Treetop, anyway? Celeste asked the first time she heard my father call me this. We were nine years old, and Celeste was my new best friend. She had moved to New Hampshire from New York City. She was tall and brown and beautiful. Her mother had modeled for magazines.

The first time I asked him where babies came from, he said Treetops.

Celeste squinted, pulled her lips to the side. I had practiced doing this in the mirror, but it never looked all the amazing things hers looked.

You know that's not true, right?

Yeah. Of course. But the name stuck.

My dad would never say that, Celeste told me. *He'd say Look it up. But he'd never call me Look It Up. Just saying.*

We laughed. From the moment we became friends, it seemed we spent so much of our time laughing.

She told me her father spent his days figuring out what to do with other people's money. *He likes counting it,* she said. *And recounting and recounting. He's tall like me,* she said. She said her parents were taking a break from each other. *After all, eleven years is a long time to be together, don't you think?*

I shrugged. When my mother died, she and my father had been together twenty years. They had been middle school sweethearts. My father said he couldn't imagine living without her.

I didn't tell Celeste this. I didn't say, *The people who don't want breaks sometimes get them*. But maybe she saw something in the way I stared at the ground. We were at the park, which was empty and cold. We were dragging our feet below our swings, moving slowly back and forth.

You miss her, huh?

I nodded.

I miss my dad, Celeste said. *And I miss New York. I know me some missing.*

I looked up and she was smiling. Then we were laughing again. That quickly, we were looking at each other and laughing so hard we had to bend over, nearly falling out of our swings.

❄

I had never known anyone brown, and Celeste had never lived in a place where brown people didn't.

It's Negro-less, she said, smiling. *It's a Negro-free zone.*

I thought we didn't say that word anymore.

Celeste looked at me. *You can't, but I can. It's in the language rulebook, I swear.*

You're lying, right? There isn't really a language rule book.

Nope. Not lying. There're all kinds of rule books. The New Hampshire rule book says only one family that's not white can live here at a time. When I move away, another family will come, I swear. It's in the rule book!

Celeste looked at me a moment. Then smiled. *I swear.*

But you're not going to move away. I wasn't smiling.

Not tomorrow.

That was the year my other friends disappeared. One by one they wanted to know why, when we had all been friends since forever, I needed this new friend now.

The one black person my mother knew stole stuff, Casey said.

They love rap music, Lisabeth said. *Does she teach you dances?*

Celeste plays piano, I said quietly. *She's been playing since she was small. Beethoven! She can play Beethoven.*

The others and I were still friends then, our dolls between our laps, their blond hair getting wrapped into braids and curls and cut and dyed. I sat in their pink bedrooms, the rooms I'd sat in for as long as I could sit alone and listened without knowing what to say back.

It hurts here and here, I was thinking. And I don't know why it hurts. But it does.

Aren't you scared? they asked. *She might take things from you. She might have a gun. Or a knife. Her feet are big. Her hair is strange. There was one at our school once, you remember? She was adopted or something, that's all I remember.*

My mom said I shouldn't eat with the new one. You shouldn't either.

Celeste arrived long after the doctors told my mother there was nothing they could do, and at night my father sat behind the bathroom door gulping back sobs. She arrived long after we buried my mother, my father and me at the graveside, our gloved hands locked together, Lisabeth and Casey behind me, standing between their own parents, safe from cancer and dead parents and holes opened in the ground. Celeste arrived in the late winter . . . and smiled at me.

Your mom would be mad if she knew, Lisabeth and Casey said.

❋

Celeste pulled me through town making me name the trees we passed—white birch, barberry, sugar maple, catalpa . . .

How do you do that? she asked again and again. *How do you know?*

Black walnut, beech, oak, pine, I said, because I loved the feeling of her hand in mine, loved the surprising softness. I didn't tell her I had never touched a black person before and how surprised I was the first time I touched her hair. But the second time I reached for it, Celeste's hand shot up, caught mine just inches from her head.

Stop! she said once when I was reaching for her hair. *I'm not a dog to be petted!*

The following autumn, we buried Celeste's pet rabbit Joe in her backyard, sprinkling crushed leaves over his tiny grave. We had been friends for close to a year and some-where in that time had grown to the same height, wore our jeans rolled at the ankle, and tied our shirts in matching knots at our waists. Celeste wore her hair out, an amazing black halo floating over her head. I had learned to keep my hands out of it, but at school, she was constantly slapping the other kids' hands away. Some mornings, when she thought no one was looking, I saw her face dip into a sadness I had only seen on my father. Those days, I wanted to grab her hand and hold on tight. But we were eleven. What did we know about anything?

Spring came again. *I like you, Treetop,* Celeste said to me one morning. *But I don't like it here.*

But you love the leaves. And egg creams!

My mom said we'd give it a year. It's been more than a year, Celeste said. She wouldn't look at me. And then, finally, she did. *New York is only four and a half hours away.*

I know.

But we both knew—the distance between New Hampshire and New York was forever away. A whole lifetime.

Celeste laced her fingers inside of mine. *The way our fingers go,* she said, *brown, white, brown, white . . . It's like the same God or Mother Nature or Universe that decided to make the leaves here all crazy colored said this*—she held up our hands—*this is right, too.*

❁

Some afternoons, Lisabeth and Casey meet me at the pharmacy on Main Street and the three of us sit at the window where we can watch people moving through town. Before she moved back, Celeste and I made a promise that we'd meet in New York City and celebrate our eighteenth birthdays together. In a week, I'll be twelve. It'll be here before you know it, Celeste said.

Why are you squinting? Lisabeth asks me. *You act like you're not even here.*

And she's right. I am already leaving. I am halfway gone.

Flying Lessons

SOMAN CHAINANI

Nani wears a fur coat to the beach.

It's my second clue she doesn't plan to go swimming.

The first came earlier this morning when she rang up the Chanel boutique on Passeig de Gràcia and asked them to send a selection of swim trunks for a young boy of twelve "with practically no hips and a small bottom" to room 213 at the Palacio Barcelona.

Half-asleep, I slid up in bed, swaddled in a voluminous white robe monogrammed with the hotel's initials, and peered up at my grandmother. Posed imperiously at the window, she was already done up in a matador-red chiffon dress, her dyed caramel hair teased into a beehive, her brown eyes drenched in blue mascara and her lips coated the color of blood.

I could hear the Chanel clerk through the handset, trying to get a word in, but Nani was prattling away: "Something stylish and sophisticated, of course. Whatever *los chicos* are wearing in Ibiza," she breezed, unaware of how ludicrous Spanglish sounded in an Indian accent. "Though nothing in black. Only Italians wear black to swim—"

"Aren't you getting a bathing suit too?" I started, but Nani waved me off, gypsy bangles jangling on her wrist.

On the bed table, there was a gilded tray of two *cafés con leche,* ham and cheese croissants, and *tostadas* slathered in tomatoes and olive oil. Nani's coffee cup was already drained.

"And please be *rápido* about it," she was saying. "It's my grandson's first trip out of Florida, and I can't have him spending the entire day in the hotel—"

Through the phone, I heard the clerk huffing that Chanel doesn't carry men's clothes, let alone swim trunks, let alone deliver them to tourists at hotels, but Nani simply smiled like a cat. "Tell Armando that Kamla Sani says hello," she replied, and hung up the phone.

Three hours later, I'm chasing Nani across the sun-drenched shores of La Mar Bella, wearing a striped Chanel red-and-white swimsuit so tiny and tight I keep peeking down to make sure it's still there, while Nani sweeps across the golden sand in her couture dress, red stiletto heels, and a white fur coat that make her look like the Indian version of Cruella de Vil.

"You promised to take me to the beach!" I yell.

"And I am. You didn't say anything about *staying* with you," Nani calls, shielded by enormous Paloma Picasso sunglasses.

"But I don't know anyone here, and my Spanish is terrible! You can't leave me in the middle of nowhere all alone—"

"It's a beach, not an alleyway in Las Ramblas. I'm just getting a wash-and-blow at Rossano Ferretti and meeting an old acquaintance at Café Gijón. I won't be more than a few hours."

"A few hours! What do you expect me to do with a few hours?"

"What any boy your age should do on a beach in Spain. Make *friends*," she impels as we approach a crowded inlet. "Here we are. Yamila at the hotel told me this is where the most exclusive people go."

I can feel the bodies around me, but I can't bear to look at them. "Please. Don't leave me alone. I'll come with you. . . ."

But she's already sashaying away. "Making friends is easy. I do it all the time."

Heart hammering, I glance up at the packed beach, finally seeing the people around me. My stomach implodes.

"Grandma!" I cry.

She turns on her heel, alarmed.

"They're *naked*!" I scream. "You brought me to a naked beach!"

Nani gapes at me, then raises her eyes and pulls down her sunglasses. As she takes in the sea of bodies, her almond skin blanches, tight wrinkles creasing her forehead. She's a hawk caught in a trap.

But then her eyes float down to me, quivering in my Speedo like a spooked starlet, and she pulls up her sunglasses with a stern smile.

"Oh, my little darling. You have such an imagination," she coos, and glides away without looking back.

Nani never asked if I wanted to go on this trip. She just flounced into our kitchen at eight a.m. on a scorching June morning, wearing a Dior sweat suit, drinking a Power Greens juice, and extolling the virtues of Pilates, before informing my mother she was taking me on a three-week trip across Europe and that I'd need a passport, haircut, and a new wardrobe that wasn't from Old Navy. She never addressed my two brothers, who were eating breakfast with me, nor explained to me why I was the one chosen for this foreign tour, nor allowed my mother a say in the matter. She just drained her juice, gave our plates of soggy French toast a pitying glare, and jaunted out of the house.

Less than a month later, I am alone on a naked beach.

When we started this trip, I thought it would be a packed itinerary of cultural landmarks: guided ferries down the

Thames, tours of the Prado and Eiffel Tower, afternoon tea at Dutch brasseries while I got ahead on my summer reading for school. Instead, I haven't seen a single museum or palace or anything else we learned about in Ms. Fisher's class, and I'm pretty sure Nani secretly threw out my summer reading books during a customs search in Copenhagen.

In Berlin, she left me stranded in the middle of a dodgy parade. In Marseilles, she paid a fast-talking young cab-driver named Gael to take me out with his wild teenage friends while she shopped for shoes. And yesterday, on our first night in Spain, I dressed up in a suit and combed my hair so I'd look nice for the "theater," only to end up cowering in the front row at an adults-only burlesque.

Why can't I have a normal grandmother? Why is every second of this trip a walk off the gangplank?

Nani returns to the beach four hours later in a completely new dress and hairstyle and finds me hiding in a dank, foul-smelling cave, knees balled to my chest.

"Have you really been in here the whole time?" She frowns.

"This is pointless," I mumble. "All of this is *pointless*."

"It's true." Nani sighs, eyeing my new swimsuit. "If I knew you'd spend the whole day in the dark, you could have just worn your underpants instead."

I give her the silent treatment all the way back to the hotel.

* * *

"Did you take Mom away too when she was young?" I ask later, struggling to crack a stone crab at dinner.

"Your mother is like your grandfather," Nani says vaguely, already finished shelling and eating hers.

"What's that mean?" I ask, trying to keep the slippery crab in the silver cracker.

"They'd rather stay home and do work."

"Yeah, but that's how they both make money—"

"And what do they *do* with it?" Nani fires. "Your mother hoards every dime as if she'll live forever. Your grandfather hasn't taken me to a movie or dinner or show or anywhere else in fifteen years. 'We're old now,' he says. 'We're old.'"

"But he lets you spend as much money as you want—"

"Money!" She pounces. "What good is money to a bird in a *cage*?"

Her eyes glow with emotion. For the first time, I can't find Nani inside of them.

Slowly her gaze softens. Her hands unclench. "Santosh, sweetie. You really sat there in that dark cave the whole afternoon?"

"What was I supposed to do? Enjoy the *scenery*?"

"By the time I came back, the beach was teeming with families," says Nani, taking a big swig of champagne. "You were so busy worrying about naked aunties that you didn't notice all the kids your age running around, looking as friendly as could be."

I give up on the crab. "Can't we just visit the Basilica Sagrada like other Americans?"

She puts down her glass. "Do you know why I brought you on this trip, Santosh?"

"So you could get away from Grandpa?"

She lets out a cackle. "No! Well, yes. But no. I brought you on this trip because you win too many awards at school."

I stare at her blankly. "What?"

"Best in math, best in English, best in debate, history, science, chorus . . . How many awards can you win? Every year I come to the ceremony and watch you go back and forth to the stage, picking up all the trophies and making me and your mother carry them, because there are too many for you to hold."

"Nani," I say, losing patience. "What does winning awards have to do with anything?"

"Because when you're older, no one cares how many awards you win, Santosh. People care if you have something to talk about. And right now, all you have to talk about are things from books."

My cheeks are hot. I'm pretty sure that my nani—my sixty-nine-year-old nani—is calling me a nerd. Not just a nerd, but a nerd who doesn't have a life, who has no friends, who is a complete and total loser. The cool boys at school taunt me the same way, with their perfect faces and athletic bodies and 20/20 eyes. But it doesn't matter what they say. Because every year at the last assembly, they and their parents have to sit there and watch me win every single last award while they win nothing, nada, zilch, and they'll continue to watch me win every last award until senior year, when I'm valedictorian and I go to Harvard and I have a *real* life while they look back and realize that I was the cool kid all along and *they* were the losers. So for Nani—the one person who I look up to more than anyone in this world, the one person who is supposed to love me unconditionally—to now say the same thing as the hot boys at school . . .

She sees it in my face.

"I used to love seeing you win all those awards, Santosh. I loved seeing you and your mother happy," she says softly. "But now when you win, you don't smile anymore. The more you win, the less happy you look."

Heat rips through me, and I turn away. "I'll be happy when I get home from this *trip*."

A long pause stretches between us. I can feel my jaw clamped shut.

Nani's hand gently touches mine. "Santosh, all I'm asking is that for the last two days of our trip, I want you to forget about books and trophies and school—"

"You don't know me, okay?" I retort, but my voice fades

as I say it, and for once Nani lets me piddle with my crab in silence.

The next day, I ask to go back to the beach.

Nani seems to have anticipated this, because my swim trunks have been steam-cleaned and she's already made her own plans for the day, which include a manicure at the Pink Peony and lunch with old friends at La Tetereria.

Before we depart, she stuffs my backpack with a bag of dried mango, two bottles of Pellegrino, and her La Roche-Posay sunscreen—though when I try to slip in a book I bought at the shop yesterday, she sighs so defeatedly that I give up and leave it behind.

This time, she asks Yamila to direct us to a beach more "child-appropriate" and we end up at Nova Icària, an S-shaped curve of hot gold sand sloping down to coral-green water. Nani buys me a vanilla ice cream cone (*"Vanilla?"* she jabs. "When they have olive, saffron, or mascarpone?") and watches as I slink out to the sand, before she gives me a last reassuring smile and hustles away.

I forgot to bring a towel, so I wince as I sit down in smoldering sand, a fair distance from the sea and the kids swimming in it. There doesn't seem to be anyone here over the age of sixteen. A few lanky, deep-tanned boys are on each other's shoulders, playing chicken, while another group of them try to do handstands in shallow water. Girls hang out in giggly packs, inspecting the boys. Those that aren't with their friends are in couples, splashing, wrestling, whispering, and kissing. Nobody is alone.

Except me.

It should be easy to make friends. Nani does it. My brothers do it. Everyone does it, as if it's as normal as eating, sleeping, breathing. I remind myself that it's natural to be on my own in a foreign country, but even if I were on the beach two miles from my house, I'd be sitting solo in the exact same spot with my melting vanilla. It's like there's a chromosome for fun I didn't get. ("The ball and chain," my younger brother's friend once murmured as I left the room.)

It's almost as if without knowing it, I made some deal with the devil: I can have all the success in the world, but no one will ever like me.

I don't want that deal anymore.

I want to unmake it.

Dear God, please help me, and I promise I'll—

A ball hits me in the chest.

It's red and small and pegs me so hard and fast that tears coat my eyes and I can't breathe.

I see a boy running toward me.

He's blurred, so I can't make out more than his tall frame and a round wooden paddle in his hand, and for a second

I think he hit me on purpose and now he's going to hit me with the paddle—

But then I see his hand over his mouth, his cheeks a shamed pink.

"*¿Estás bien?*" he says, panting. "*Lo siento, lo siento. . . .*"

I don't answer because: (a) I'm still winded; (b) I can't say, "*No, no bien*—my chest hurts, I'm crying in front of strangers, and I dropped ice cream on my privates" in Spanish, and most of all, (c) I'm still scared of him.

He has wavy black hair, honey-gold skin, jade-green eyes, and looks the way I always imagined Romeo would look when we read *Romeo and Juliet* in Mrs. Gonzalez's class. He can't be more than a couple years older than me.

"*¿Estás bien?*" Romeo repeats, kneeling down and clutching my arm. "*Estamos jugando y . . .*"

He points at two other handsome boys and a skinny girl down the shore, watching us, each holding an identical wooden paddle and waiting for their friend to finish apologizing and bring back the ball.

The boy's eyes fall on my backpack. "Ahhhh, Americano," he says, touching the Delta luggage tag.

"Americano in pain," I mumble, rubbing the welt on my chest.

To my surprise he laughs—either because he knows some English or he's relieved I'm responsive. Then Romeo looks around and sees there's no one within twenty feet of me.

His thick brows furrow and he studies my face so intensely and curiously that I lose my breath again.

"*¿Quieres jugar?*" he asks, and holds out his paddle.

My stomach flips.

Want to play?

Romeo, oh Romeo, just asked me if I want to play.

Do you know the number of times I've fantasized about being asked this exact question while watching boys hang out with their friends?

My hand's sweating.

Take it.

Take it now!

I feel myself reaching for the paddle—

"Tomas! *¡Apurate!*"

I turn and see his friends beckoning him, their eyes shifted away from me.

Tomas. That's his real name.

And his friends want him back.

They don't want me to play.

Tomas doesn't either, of course. He's only asked me to be nice and absolve himself of guilt for pelting a lonely tourist.

I look up into his shiny green eyes and gently push the paddle toward him.

"*Adiós,*" I say, expecting him to look relieved to be rid of me.

But he doesn't look relieved.

He looks . . . hurt.

As he lopes back to his friends and resumes his game, I have the sinking feeling that Tomas wasn't trying to get rid of me at all. He wanted to make a new friend and I just rejected him the way I thought he was rejecting me.

That's what I do every time. That's why I'm always alone.

It doesn't matter, I grouse, fumbling for the dried mango in my bag and trying to forget about Tomas, this beach, this entire trip.

As I gnaw on the orange shreds, I think about how much better my summer reading essay will be than everyone else's. I think about a science fair project that will make State Finals. I think about how this year I'll win more trophies than ever before. . . .

But none of it makes me feel happy.

It makes me feel worse.

I tell Nani I made friends. That I had a great time.

"Did you?" she says, sounding surprised as we slide into a taxi. "Well, you must want to come back tomorrow, then."

"No, it's okay," I say quickly. "It's our last day tomorrow. Let's do something else."

She doesn't reply.

Two hours later, we're standing side by side in a vast, smoky kitchen that reeks of olives and Iberian ham.

I'd asked her if we could go somewhere less fancy for dinner tonight. Somewhere that wasn't filled with rich, old couples.

This is my punishment.

"Santosh, you'll have to chop a little faster if you want our dish to actually be *served*," says Nani, dressed in a sequined pantsuit as she stirs the paella rice.

I look up at all the other teams at their cooking stations, hovering over their *patatas bravas, boquerones,* and *paquetitos.* It's an authentic Catalan cooking class, taught entirely in Spanish, so Nani and I only catch every eighth word. ("Couldn't you have asked Yamila for something taught in English?" I growl. "And cook with *tourists*?" she flares.)

Nani commandeers our paella—she's both a brilliant cook and quite competitive, already throwing darting looks at the other teams—while she leaves me the lone task of chopping the shrimp. So far I've managed to slice three of them. My mind is still somewhere on the beach.

"You don't think they have garam masala, do you?" I hear Nani saying. "Or at least some red chilies . . ."

I ignore her.

"By the way, what were the names of the friends you made?"

I snap out of my stupor and see her sprinkling parsley over the pan.

"What?"

"I asked you the names of your friends," she repeats, not looking at me.

"Oh, I can't remember," I say, suddenly focused on my shrimp. "They were complicated names. Spanish ones."

"I see. And what did you do with these nameless friends?"

"Swam and played ball. Usual stuff. You should put the mussels in, Nani. I think he said to put those in before the—"

"Did you speak to them in Spanish or English?"

"I don't see what—"

She glares at me. "Or did you sit in the same spot for two hours, watching a boy play ball with his friends after that very same boy offered you a chance to join in and you *refused*?"

I gawk at her, eyes wide. Then I notice her hands. Hands bearing yesterday's nail polish. Hands that never made it to the Pink Peony.

"You were *spying* on me?" I yell.

The whole kitchen goes quiet. Teams leer at us, their dishes already plated.

Nani and I shove a lid on our furies and finish the paella.

Well, Nani finishes. I just stew.

Neither of us speak in the taxi ride back to the hotel, which is fine by me, because my stomach feels like a kettlebell. I should have pretended to eat the other teams' plates, like Nani did, and just made do with the olives and prosciutto.

"I wasn't spying on you, Santosh," she says finally. "I felt bad you spent yesterday in a cave, so today when I dropped you off, I waited to make sure you were okay. Then that boy hit you with his ball and I was about to run down into the sand and give him a beating . . . but then I saw you talking to him. He even held out the racket, as if he wanted you to play. When you pushed it away, I thought it was because you don't like sports. Your mother hates sports too. Like your grandfather. But then instead of going for a walk or swimming or buying more ice cream, you just sat there, staring at that boy after he left. I waited so long for you to get up that I almost missed my lunch. But you never moved."

My stomach cramps tighter. I can feel my armpits sweating. "I wasn't staring at him," I say coldly.

She smiles at me. "The wonderful thing about Europe is that you can stare at whoever you like and no one cares."

I don't smile back. "Grandma. *I wasn't staring at him.*"

The poison in my voice is so toxic the lightness vanishes from her face.

Nani nods, biting at the edge of her lip, before she peers through her window and I turn to look out mine.

I relish the silence.

"Though it's a funny thing," she says. "At your age, sometimes it's hard to know whether you like someone . . . or whether you just want to *be* them."

I turn sharply, but her eyes are locked out the window, where they stay for the rest of the ride.

The next morning, I can still feel dinner sitting in my stomach.

Nani has some last-minute shopping to do, so I tell her I'm going to read in the park until lunch. But I don't go to the park. Instead, I slip my still-wet swimsuit under my shorts and ask pretty, bubbly Yamila at the concierge desk to call me a taxi to the beach. She looks a touch wary of sending me off on my own, but I smile and tell her Nani's sleeping and it seems to do the trick.

An hour later, I'm in my usual spot, clutching vanilla ice cream and watching Tomas down the shore, tanning in the sun next to the skinny blond girl who'd been playing paddleball with him the day before.

Tomas spotted me when I arrived. He craned his head, his eyes flicking over my toothpick frame before he yawned and lay back down on his towel.

He didn't look at me after that.

Blond Girl nudges him in the chest and says something that makes him laugh.

I hate that girl.

I hate her stupid blond hair and stupid mousy face.

Hot guilt flushes through me.

That girl is his *friend*. She actually *knows* Tomas. I don't. And I hate her why?

Why am I even here? What did I think would happen if I came back to the beach? That I'd get a do-over? That Tomas would hit me with a ball again and ask me to play? Or that he'd bound over and say hi like we're best friends?

You're not just a loser, I think. *You're delusional. You're sick—*

"Hello, darling," chimes a singsong voice, and I look up sharply to see a striking older woman barrel by in a glittering gold one-piece swimsuit, a hotel towel wrapped around her head like a turban. "Getting your reading done, I see."

"Nani?" I chase her, hopping like a frog because the sand is so hot. "What are you doing here?"

"Yamila called me, knowing full well I don't sleep late, and told me a cabdriver dropped you at the beach," she wisps. "If only you'd given me a bit more time to get my hair done . . . Luckily, I found a swimsuit at the hotel boutique that didn't look too tawdry. I hope your friend likes it."

"Nani, look, I just wanted to . . . Wait. What friend?"

But now I see where Nani is walking. She's headed straight for Tomas.

"No—no—no—no," I stammer, but she trips me with a swift kick and I face-plant in sand as she motors ahead.

"Better keep up, darling," I hear her chirp.

I scramble to my feet, staggering after her, but she's closing in on Tomas now. He's raising his neck . . . he's looking at her . . . he's looking at me right behind her, and just as he and Nani make eye contact—

Nani faints.

She crumples to the ground in Tomas's lap, so exquisitely, so dramatically, that I know at once I'm doomed.

In a flash, Tomas props up Nani's head, while Blond Girl flutters about in useless panic. I stay right where I am, scowling with arms crossed, fully aware of what's coming next.

Nani's eyelids crack open. "Santosh? Santosh, sweetie pie?" she rasps with a quivery lip, playing it so thick she practically holds for applause. "Santosh, where are you?"

"Right here, Lady Macbeth," I snap, glowering down at her.

Tomas looks up at me, confused. "*¿Concoces?*"

I'm about to say, No, I've never seen this woman in my life, and run for the parking lot, but Nani preempts me by lifting herself gingerly and clinging to Tomas's arm like a raft.

"Come, Santosh, darling," she wheezes, adding a few hacking coughs, as if while fake fainting she also happened to contract tuberculosis. "Stay with your nani and this handsome boy who rescued me."

Nani stabs out her hand, seizes my wrist, and with the

strength of a sumo wrestler, drags me down into the sand next to Tomas, boxing Blond Girl out completely.

"*Agua . . . ,*" she heaves to the girl, as if on her last breaths. "*Necesito . . . agua . . .*"

Blond Girl wrinkles her little freckled nose at me as if getting the woman water should be *my* job since I'm the one who knows her, but Tomas clears his throat and glares at her until she lets out an audible huff and stomps off.

Nani musters another ludicrous cough. "Now let me have a rest, while you two boys get to know each other," she says, before laying her head on Tomas's shoulder and gripping him by the waist, as if to trap him in place.

Tomas looks at me wide-eyed.

Yesterday, he hit me with a ball. Today, I hit him with Nani.

I snicker at the thought. Tomas snorts too, though again, I'm not sure what he's laughing at.

"*Soy* Tomas," he says finally.

"*Soy* Santosh," I say.

"Santosh Americano." He smiles.

I nod, blushing hot pink. "Santosh Americano."

An hour later, I know a lot more about Tomas. For starters, he's thirteen. The blond girl is his sister Karolina, whom he finds a bit clingy and annoying. (Indeed, he doesn't intervene when she comes back with water and Nani orders her away again to get ice cream.) He lives in Barcelona, but he wants to go to college in America (either Duke or UCLA). He's hoping to become a sports therapist—the kind that run onto soccer fields when a goalie hurts his knee, he says—but he doesn't like American food, so he jokes that if he comes to America, he needs someone who can make him Spanish meals. (Nani jolts up from her slumber to say she'll teach me to cook for him, but I elbow her hard and she closes her eyes.) He likes jazz music, *Lord of the Rings*, and bike riding, and his favorite movie is *Aliens*.

I lie and tell Tomas I'm thirteen, so he doesn't think I'm lame, but that's the only lie I tell. He knows I like Taylor Swift, E. M. Forster books, and tennis (I like Federer; he likes Nadal), and my favorite movie is *Jurassic Park*. I tell him stories about me and Nani's trip—he cracks up when I say she left me at La Mar Bella—and he says he wishes he had a grandmother as cool as mine. (Nani's lips curl into a smile.)

We talk in our own chaotic Spanglish: a fluid version of English, Spanish, and body language that makes absolutely no sense, and yet we understand each other completely.

I never mention school.

I never even think about school.

Karolina returns, holding a cup of dark green ice cream, but this time she's accompanied by a plump, grumpy old woman I take to be her grandmother, as if the only way to defuse my nani is with one of her own.

Tomas's face clouds over, as if Grump Granny's presence can only mean one thing: it's time for him to go.

"*¿Hasta mañana?*" he asks, looking into my eyes.

I shake my head miserably, about to tell him I'm going home—

"*Hasta mañana,*" Nani interjects, patting Tomas's back as she pulls off him.

He looks right at me with a smile so happy and hopeful that my heart swells at the seams, throbbing against my ribs until I see the last of his shadow disappear behind a sandy slope.

"Why did you lie to him?" I turn to Nani. "Why did you tell him I'd see him tomorrow?"

The mischief evaporates from her face. Instead, there's a veil of sadness, as if I've woken her from a beautiful dream. Nani doesn't look vibrant and carefree anymore. She looks . . . old.

"To give him something to look forward to, Santosh," she says quietly, before gazing out at the sea. "All of us need something to look forward to."

I nestle into her arms as we watch the crash and spray of waves. Her arms are so warm I don't want her to let go.

"Will you take me on another trip next year, Nani?" I ask, tight with emotion.

"Oh, Santosh, don't you see?" she whispers, glassing with tears. "You're the one taking me."

For a moment, I don't understand . . . and yet somewhere in my heart I do.

We're the same, Nani and I.

Two caged birds, searching for a way out.

"Shouldn't leave it behind," she says, nodding at the cup of half-melted ice cream in the sand next to me.

The surface glints in the sun, dark and emerald as a forest.

It's the same color as Tomas's eyes.

"Go on, then," I hear Nani whisper.

I slip a spoonful into my mouth and sweetness and tartness riot inside me, lighting my heart on fire.

Gasping, I turn back—

But Nani's gone, and for a second, I look up, thinking she's flown away.

Seventy-Six Dollars and Forty-Nine Cents
A STORY-IN-VERSE

KWAME ALEXANDER

HOW TO WRITE A MEMOIR

After reading
"Oranges"
by Gary Soto
(who I like)
Mr. Preston
(who I don't)
asks us
if we liked it
(which I did)
then makes us
write
(which I hate)
our own memoirs.
Now, make it interesting
(which I'm not)
he adds, looking dead
at me.

QUESTION ABOUT THE ASSIGNMENT

I know memoir is
based in fact, but can it have
a little fiction?

MY NAME IS MONK

which is not a terrible name
(but certainly not a cool one).

Every single minute
of every single school day

I am two letters away
from suffering

through the same lame jokes:

"What's up, MonkEY?"
"What's up, FUnk?"

I can thank my mom for that.
You see, when she went

into labor with me,
she was listening to

"Round Midnight"
by Thelonious Monk

I guess it could have been worse.
She could have been reading *Moby-Dick*.

ONCE UPON A TIME

I was uncool.

Useless.

An empty pool in the summer.

A pencil with no lead.

Macaroni without cheese.

You get the point. . . .

I was nothing.

A nobody.

That was before.

I WAS THE KID

who spent his weekends
reading Star Wars books
and magazines
and reciting lines
from each movie
with my best friend
and fellow Star Wars junkie,
Hervé, who
mows lawns
with me
so we can make money
to buy more
Star Wars books
so we can picture
ourselves as Han Solo
or Luke Skywalker
flying off to some
far-off universe
to rescue
my wonder woman:
Angel Carter.

ANGEL CARTER

should be a speeding ticket
'cause she is *Fine*.

THE POINT IS

I've never been cool.
The closest I've come
to having a girlfriend
was last year
when this sixth grader
smiled at me with
her pearly-white gap teeth
and asked if she could see
my homework.
I said okay, she copied it, then
split like a perpendicular bisector
through an acute triangle.
No more smiles after that.
Just the same ol' boring,
uncool life that I've been living
for the past 12 years.
Until something amazing occurred.
I don't exactly know how
I got to be the lucky one.
But I can tell you when it happened.

MY FATHER, JACK JACKSON,

is in the Air Force.
Most folks call him *Major*.
When Mom's mad at him
(like when he doesn't put the toilet seat down),
she calls him Major *JackASS*.

We've lived all over the country,
and once in Bermuda
where I met Lisa Castillo
the first crush
of my life.

LISA CASTILLO

My memory of her
is a little vague.
I was eight.

She was about the same age,
I think, but shorter, maybe.
She wore white, or was it green.

Like I said, I only met her once,
on the beach, but I could tell
by the way she threw sand

in my eyes
that she felt the same way
about me.

I've had a complicated history
with girls.

SO, HERE'S WHEN IT HAPPENED

We were in Dad's
red Ford Thunderbird
on the New Jersey Turnpike
listening to *Harry Potter* on tape
when all of a sudden
Dad falls asleep
(while he's driving)
and Mom yells *JAAACKKK!*
which wakes me and my sister up
and jolts Dad back to life
just in enough time
for him to avoid swerving
into the eighteen-wheeler
beside us,
but not before I bang
my head against
the armrest
in front of me.
(Yeah, I know, I shoulda had my seat belt on. . . .)

After he apologizes
Mom makes him pull off
at the Thomas Edison Rest Area

which is kind of ironic
since Edison's last breath
is supposedly contained
in a test tube
at the Henry **Ford** Museum.

31 FLAVORS

While Dad
power-naps
in the car,
Mom treats us to
ice cream:

Little Sister: *Bubble Gum Ice Cream
with Sprinkles* (Waffle cone, of course.)
Mom: *Lime and Strawberry Sherbet*
(She's lactose-intolerant.)
Me: *A Thick Super-Size Chocolate Double Fudge
Milk Shake* (With two straws.)

HEADACHE

I don't know if it was
the banging of my head
or sipping the shake
too fast, but
I get hit hard
with a sharp head pain
that travels down
my neck and back
to my toes, and then, oddly,
back up to my head,
and I feel like
I'm in a cartoon,
'cause I see stars
(but my eyes are wide open,
so I close 'em),
and then a sharp blue light
shoots through
the darkness
and my eyes jolt open.
Then everything's
back to normal.

Or so I think.

SO, HERE'S WHAT HAPPENED

"Monk, are you okay? You're shivering."

"I'm fine, Mom."

"All right, well, finish up, we've got to get moving,"
    she says, and then she says something else,
    but her lips aren't moving.

> *This sherbet is disgusting.*
> *Milk or no milk, next time*
> *I'm getting French vanilla ice cream.*

"You want me to order you something else, Ma?" I ask.

"What are you talking about, Monk? I'm fine."

"But I thought you just said—?"

"I didn't know dummies could think," says my annoying
    sister,

right before Mom

slaps her on the hand.

"I've told you about using that word, young lady."

"Sorry, Mom," and then she says something else,
    but her lips aren't moving, either.

Why is she always picking on me?
Monk's her favorite. I hate him.

And now they're both talking,
and their mouths are shut.
WHAT. IS. GOING. ON?

I better drive, 'cause Jack almost killed us.
I want a dog.

And they just keep talking,
or thinking (out loud),
back and forth, and
I just sit there, speechless,
looking
and listening, and
it's scary
and funny
at the same time.

UNBELIEVABLE

When we get back
to the car,
I text Hervé,
who naturally
doesn't believe me
when I tell him
I can hear
other people's thoughts
when I'm looking
at them.
"Bet you ten dollars I can," I tell him.
"Make it twenty, sucker," he responds.
"Bet, and I'll prove it," I text, "soon as
we get back to school
on Monday."

MONDAYS ARE QUIZ DAY

in Mr. Olley's science class.
I always ace them, but that was
before I had a superpower to practice
all weekend instead of studying biology.

Mr. Olley doesn't give multiple-choice
and true/false quizzes
like most teachers at Greenwood Middle.
This dude gives essay questions. (Lame.)

There are always two items
on each quiz that he wants us
to explain in great detail:
one paragraph per answer.

Most students only get
one right, 'cause there's just
so many possibilities and
it's hard to study

if you haven't been paying attention
in class, like, uh, most students.
To be fair to Mr. Olley,
he does give us one last chance

to pass.
Five minutes before the quiz
he stands

in front of the class
and answers
our last-minute questions
about anything

we studied
the previous week.
Just like *Jeopardy*.
I ask Hervé if he's ready
for me to prove

that I can read
minds. He nods.
Here we go.

GAME ON!

JEOPARDY

I walk
to Olley's desk
to ask him
something bogus
about extra credit
or something,
when Hervé, just like
we planned,
raises his hand
to get Mr. Olley's attention.

"Yes, Hervé?"
"Mr. Olley, I was wondering
if you could tell us
what's on the quiz today?"
Everyone in the class gets quiet.
Mr. Olley looks up, smiles,
and continues
listening to me
yap about extra credit.
I'm staring right at him, and
that's when I hear him:

Kids these days. If they just studied
instead of playing those video games,
maybe they'd be better prepared.
Mitosis and DNA. Easy stuff,
if you bothered to study.

"Monk, I really need to get class started.
You don't need the extra credit,
but come by after school and
I'll have an assignment for you."

"Thanks, Mr. Olley," I tell him.
I wink at Hervé
on the way
to my seat.
"Okay, class, you know what time it is," Olley says.
"Get out your pencils for the quiz."

"Mr. Olley, aren't you forgetting something?" Hervé asks.
"Yeah, Olley, we didn't do the *Jeopardy!* thang," another
    student hollers.
"Very well, class, let's give it a go."
Olley picks his stopwatch off the desk.
"You have five minutes. Anything goes.
On your mark, get set, go!"

"Olley, what's your sign? Are you a Sagittarius or a
Capricorn?"
Everyone laughs except me.

"Four minutes and twenty seconds left," Olley says,
yawning.
"Mr. Olley, are cell membranes fluid?"
No, no, don't ask that, I think. It's not on the quiz.
"Yes, they are. Three minutes, fourteen seconds," he says,
grinning.

Time to put my magic to work.
"Mr. Olley?"
"Yes, Monk?"
"Can you remind us of the phases of Mitosis?"

Lucky guess.

"Mitosis is nuclear division plus cytokinesis, and
it produces two identical daughter cells during prophase,
prometaphase, metaphase, anaphase."
I smile at Hervé, then turn back to Mr. Olley.
Only one minute left.
"Mr. Olley?" He looks at me, frowning a little.
"Yes, Monk?"

I go in for the kill. . . .

THE KILL

"I know that DNA, otherwise known as
deoxyribonucleic acid, is a group of molecules
that carry the genetic information necessary
for the organization and functioning
of most living cells and control
the inheritance of certain characteristics,
but I am just not sure whether it is in every cell
in our bodies."

Olley's mouth hits
the top of his junky desk.
It's like he's just seen
the ghost
of Tupac Shakur
walk by.
I watch him
while he watches me,
wondering
what he's gonna do.

He only has a few choices.
He could give the quiz,
and 99% of us
will ace it (because

I just gave the class
the answers
to both questions),
thereby
ruining his reputation
for having
the hardest tests
in school.

Or he could
postpone the test,
save himself
the embarrassment,
and give us a makeup
on two new topics
later in the week.

Guess which one he chooses.

THE CLASS GOES WILD

You would think it's
the Fourth of July
the way everyone's celebrating.
NO QUIZ TODAY!
I can see the fireworks
going off
in Olley's baffled eyes, as he
tries to figure out
how I knew
both questions
on the pop quiz.

Thing is, using my "powers" like that
doesn't feel so great,
so after Hervé
pays me my twenty dollars, I
decide it's a onetime thing.

Or not.

AFTER CLASS

My classmates
bum-rush me,
thank me
for whatever I said or did
to make Olley cancel.

One girl, who's from Louisiana,
asks if I put a spell on him.
It's pretty cool to get all the attention,
especially from kids who
don't even know
I'm alive.
Athletes.
Cool kids.
ANGEL CARTER!

ANGEL CARTER CAPTIVATES ME

I don't know exactly why.
Maybe it's because she reminds me of Lisa Castillo.
Maybe it's because I once dreamt about her lips.
Maybe it's because when I see her
in the hallway
or the lunchroom
it's like watching
water
in the desert.

Once, I even wrote
a haiku
about her
(changing her name, of course)
for the school poetry journal.

River is a sweet
song, and one of these days, I
will carry her tune.

I signed it

Anonymous.

THERE'S ONE (BIG) PROBLEM, THOUGH

As beautiful as Angel is,
she's even more stuck up.
So nobody really likes her.
(Except me.)
We've been classmates
since fourth grade
and she's never even smiled
at me.

Some of the girls
in our class
say she thinks
she's better
than us.

When I told her
what they were saying
about her
(to get on her good side),
she whipped
her long brown hair
and replied,

"I am."

BEFORE I CONTINUE

with this memoir
I'd like to remind you
that this part
of my life
happened at my previous school
so don't try to figure out
who's who, plus
all of the names
(except mine)
have been changed
to protect
the innocent
and the guilty.

Now, back to the story . . .

SWAG

I'm standing in the hallway
getting daps and high-fives
from my classmates
when who walks up to me but,
yep, you guessed it:
ANGEL CARTER.

OH SNAP! This is the BEST. DAY. EVER!
But, wait, she doesn't look
happy.

The most beautiful girl
in school
walks up to me
fast and furious
like a wave rushing
to the shore.

I feel like
I'm about to drown,
but I don't care,
because like my dad says
about my mom,
"She's a stone cold fox!"

(I don't even know what that means,
but it sounds pretty cool.)

Her hair is braided
in hundreds of tiny cornrows, so thin
you could lace
sneakers with them.
She's wearing capris
and pink high-top Converse.
Now she's smiling. Or smirking.
Maybe she's gonna give me
my props.
When she gets near me, I hear,

> *What a lowlife.*

Who's she talking about? I wonder.
"You ain't all that, Monk. I don't even know
why everybody's sweatin' you. You're
such a geek," she says, and that's when
I realize I'm the *lowlife*
she was talking about. GEESH!

"Yeah, a geek," says Angel's best (and only) friend,
   Carla.
They laugh, then, like the tide,

go back into
the big middle school sea, and
I know I won't get
too many more chances
like this.

LAST CHANCE

"Um, Angel, maybe I am *all that*," I say nervously. "Maybe
I read Mr. Olley's mind
and knew the quiz
was gonna be on mitosis and DNA,
and that's why he canceled it."

Carla stops, turns around, and yells, "OH, NOW YOU
    GOT ESPN?" which sends
the entire hallway into raucous laughter.
Angel shakes her head. "It's ESP, girl."

And this is The Moment
when my Entire. Life. Changes.

"BET I CAN READ YOUR MIND, ANGEL," I holler,
    sweating profusely.

JEOPARDY, PART TWO

Part of me wishes she'd just
keep on walking.
The other half prays
she turns around.

Everyone is quiet.
Angel stops, drops her bag, and
marches toward my locker
like I just started
something.

> *I got to pee,* I hear her say to herself.

"Excuse me, geek? I know you're not trying
to start nothing," she says.
"I'm just saying, I know a lot more
than you think I know," I fire back.

"Okay, so just because you're smart,
you may know all the subjects and
school stuff, but you don't know stuff
that matters."

> *If he wore some better clothes, he might be kinda*
> *cute. NOT!*

"Maybe I do." Sweat drips down my neck. "Maybe
you should ask me something,
anything you want to,
and I'll tell you the answer."
Angel and Carla laugh real loud.
The other kids join in.
It's like a circus in the hall and
Angel and I are the main attractions.
"You want a question. *¿Cuál es la fecha de hoy, stupido?*"
And even though I take French
instead of Spanish,
I don't need telepathy
to know that whatever
she just asked me,
she ended with *Stupid.*
The whole hallway
is laughing at me, and
she's eating it up.

THE QUESTION

"I'm serious, Angel. Ask me a real question,
something I could never really know, and
if I get it wrong, I will do
your geometry homework
for the rest
of the month.
But if I'm right, you have to,
you have to, uh, eat lunch
with me all next week."

GEESH! I finally get
Angel Carter's attention,
and all I can think
to ask for is a measly lunch.
Maybe she's right. I am *stupido*.
Why didn't I say a movie or a hug?
(That would have been real nice.)

> *What is he doing? He's kind of strange.*
> *I think we used to go*
> *to the same elementary school.*

"All right, stupid, if you wanna
do my geometry,
it's a deal. Let me see what I can ask. . . ."

What a loser. My grandmother was born in Georgia.
He'll never know that.

"All right, Monkey,
Here's your question:
What city does my grandmother
live in?"

WAIT! City? NO FAIR!
You only said the state. GEESH!
This is not going to end well
for me.

THERE'S LIKE TWO HUNDRED

cities in Georgia.
I'll never get it right,
Unless . . .

"Angel, to be fair,
you should tell somebody
besides Carla the answer
so they can prove that I
got it when I answer it correctly."

Stalling. What a loser!

Angel whispers to some boy
who's in the orchestra with me.
I stare her down and hear it
plain and clear.

The hallway full of students sings
the *Jeopardy!* theme
song and awaits my answer.
I try to make it look good, believable.

"Well, let's see. You talk
with a little country twang
so it's gotta be a southern state.

Not Atlanta or some other big city,
else you would be bragging
about your summer vacations. So
it must be some really small town
in Alabama or Louisiana that
you're not too excited about."

I don't believe this. No way. There's no way he's
gonna get this.

"Time's up, Geek. What's your answer?"
"I'd have to say Savann—No, I think
your grandmother resides in the same
city that gave us the Godfather of Soul,
James Brown. She lives in Macon, Georgia."

Jay, the guy who plays tuba
in the Orchestra, starts running
down the hall, flashing
the paper Angel wrote
the answer on, and screaming,
"HE GOT IT! HE GOT IT! MONK'S RIGHT."

People are yelling and laughing.
Angel stands there in disbelief,
looking like Mr. Olley's twin.

I GOT THAT FEELING

"Angel, is he right?" Carla asks.
"He must have cheated or something. You
cheated, didn't you, geek? How'd
you know where my grandmamma lives?"

> *But how could he cheat?*
> *He was standing in front of me*
> *the whole time!*

"Tell you what, Angel. Since you think
I cheated, let's try it again. Double Jeopardy.
If I'm wrong, I do your homework
for the rest of the year. If I'm right,
you, uh, go to see the new *Star Wars* with me
and Hervé this weekend."

I couldn't believe I'd said that.
But I was happy I did, and I prayed
that my "powers" wouldn't leave me
before I got a chance to seal this deal.

The hallway fills with chanting:
DO IT!
    DO IT!
        DO IT!

"Angel, girl, come on, let's get out of here.
He's some kind of weirdo."

> Yeah, she's probably right, but I got something
> he can't ever know.
> I'll write it down, but I ain't whispering
> the answer to nobody either,
> 'cause he probably
> can just hear
> real good.

DO OR DIE

"All right, Monk, you think you're so cool,
but you're a fool. I'm happy to let you
do my homework
for the rest of the year."

(Hey, at least she didn't
call me stupid. That's progress, right?)

The hallway is silent, *crickets,* when
she asks her question:

"How much did my mom pay
to get my hair braided?
Including tax."

She takes out
a piece of paper, writes
the answer,
folds it up, gives
it to Carla, and walks
up to me till our noses
almost touch.

"No cheatin' this time.
What's the answer? How much?"

The hall is silent, like somebody
just took
the last shot
in a basketball game.
Will it go in?

I think we all know
the answer to that question.
Well, at least I do!

YES

I don't know why
this happened to me.
I could guess
and say maybe it was
some kind of cosmic prank, or
the universe paying me back
for so many years
of being uncool.
I don't
know for sure, but
it sure felt good
and right, and my life
would never be
the same
again.

> Oh, please don't get this.
> Please, please. I already told Justin
> I'd go see Star Wars with him
> this weekend. I gotta pee baaaad!

I knew the answer
as soon as she wrote it.
I heard her repeating it
and reassuring herself

that there was no way
I could know.
I watched her,
looked in her eyes, glassy
with fear, and
for a second I felt
sorry for her,
and I guess the nice, geeky guy in me
took over, because
I leaned into her,
and I whispered . . .

THE END

"Look, I like you,
and I would like to
go see a movie
with you someday, but only
if you really wanted to,
and plus I've kinda already got plans
with my Chewbacca Crew
to see it on Saturday, and you
and I both know
that Justin would be pissed
if you dumped him
for me,
so I'll forget
the whole bet
if you do me two favors."

Favors? Are you crazy?
Wait, how do you know about Justin?
I didn't even tell Carla
about him. OMG! Do you know?

I nod, and I can almost see
a tear forming in her eye.

"Yeah, two favors," I whisper
in her ear again, so
no one can hear us. "Uh, how about, uh, a
kiss."
"WHAT?! I don't think so!"
"It's either that, or—"
"I am not kissing you, Monk."
"Well, then, just walk me to my next class—"
"That's it?"
"And, hold my, uh . . . hand."

*Ugh! Why would I do a thing like that? I really got
to pee!*

"It's either that, or
we're going to the movies,
'cause I know
how much
your hair cost. Plus tax.
So it's your choice.
And you probably ought to decide
pretty quickly,
'cause I'd hate for you
to pee on yourself
in front of
all these people."

He knows, but how could he know?
It's not possible.
This is so embarrassing.

I back up, walk over
to my locker, and eagerly wait.

Angel Carter inches toward me
like a centipede.
When she gets so close
that her cornrows
brush up against my cardigan,
I close my eyes
and imagine
the two of us
on some tropical island,
like Bermuda, and all
I can hear is
the sound
of the cool
calm river,
and two swimmers
ready to dive.

EPILOGUE

In this memoir
I have taken
some liberties
and added a little
drama
here (and there)
to keep it *interesting*.

But everything
I've written here
is true.

(Mostly.)

Monk Oliver
Mr. Preston's Honors English 7

Sometimes a Dream Needs a Push

WALTER DEAN MYERS

You might have heard of my dad, Jim Blair. He's six five and played a year of good basketball in the pros before tearing his knee up in his second year. The knee took forever to heal and was never quite the same again. Still, he played pro ball in Europe for five years before giving it up and becoming an executive with a high-tech company.

Dad loved basketball and hoped that one day I would play the game. He taught me a lot, and I was pretty good until the accident. It was raining and we were on the highway, approaching the turnoff toward our house in Hartsdale, when a truck skidded across the road and hit our rear bumper. Our little car spun off the road, squealing as Dad tried to bring it under control. But he couldn't avoid the light pole. I remember seeing the broken windows, hearing

Mom yelling, amazingly bright lights flashing crazily in front of me. Then everything was suddenly dark. The next thing I remember is waking up in the hospital. There were surgeries and weeks in the hospital, but the important thing was that I wasn't going to be walking again.

I didn't like the idea, but Mom and I learned to live with it. Dad took it hard, real hard. He was never much of a talker, Mom said, but he talked even less since I was hurt.

"Sometimes I think he blames himself," Mom said. "Whenever he sees you in the wheelchair he wants to put it out of his mind."

I hadn't thought about that when Mr. Evans, an elder in our church, asked me if I wanted to join a wheelchair basketball team he was starting.

"We won't have the experience of the other teams in the league," he said. "But it'll be fun."

When I told Mom, she was all for it, but Dad just looked at me and mumbled something under his breath. He does that sometimes. Mom said that he's chewing up his words to see how they taste before he lets them out.

Our van is equipped with safety harnesses for my chair, and we used it on the drive to see a game between Madison and Rosedale. It was awesome to see guys my age zipping around in their chairs playing ball. I liked the chairs, too. They were specially built with rear stabilizing wheels and side wheels that slanted in. Very cool. I couldn't wait to start practicing. At the game, Mom sat next to me, but Dad went and sat next to the concession stand. I saw him reading a newspaper and only looking up at the game once in a while.

"Jim, have you actually seen wheelchair games before?" Mom asked on the way home.

Dad made a little motion with his head and said something that sounded like "Grumpa-grumpa" and then mentioned that he had to get up early in the morning. Mom looked at me, and her mouth tightened just a little.

That was okay with me because I didn't want him to talk about the game if he didn't like it. After washing and getting into my pj's I wheeled into my room, transferred to the bed, and tried to make sense of the day. I didn't know what to make of Dad's reaction, but I knew I wanted to play.

The next day at school, tall Sarah told me there was a message for me on the bulletin board. Sarah is cool but the nosiest person in school.

"What did it say?" I asked.

"How would I know?" she answered. "I don't read people's messages."

"Probably nothing important," I said, spinning my chair to head down the hall.

"Just something about you guys going to play Madison in a practice game and they haven't lost all season," Sarah said. "From Nicky G."

"Oh."

The school has a special bus for wheelchairs and the driver always takes the long way to my house, which is a little irritating when you've got a ton of homework that needs to get done, and I had a ton and a half. When I got home, Mom had the entire living room filled with purple lace and flower things she was putting together for a wedding and was lettering nameplates for them. I threw her a quick "Hey" and headed for my room.

"Chris, your coach called," Mom said.

"Mr. Evans?"

"Yes, he said your father had left a message for him," Mom answered. She had a big piece of the purple stuff around her neck as she leaned against the doorjamb. "Anything up?"

"I don't know," I said with a shrug. My heart sank. I went into my room and started on my homework, trying not to think of why Dad would call Mr. Evans.

With all the wedding stuff in the living room and Mom looking so busy, I was hoping that we'd have pizza again. No such luck. Somewhere in the afternoon she had found time to bake a chicken. Dad didn't get home until nearly seven-thirty, so we ate late.

While we ate Mom was talking about how some woman was trying to convince all of her bridesmaids to put a pink streak in their hair for her wedding. She asked us what we thought of that. Dad grunted under his breath and went back to his chicken. He didn't see the face that Mom made at him.

"By the way"—Mom gave me a quick look—"Mr. Evans called. He said he had missed your call earlier."

"I spoke to him late this afternoon," Dad said.

"Are the computers down at the school?" Mom asked.

"No, I was just telling him that I didn't think that the Madison team was all that good," Dad said. "I heard the kids saying they were great. They're okay, but they're not great. I'm going to talk to him again at practice tomorrow."

"Oh," Mom said. I could see the surprise in her face and felt it in my stomach.

The next day zoomed by. It was like the bells to change classes were ringing every two minutes. I hadn't told any of the kids about my father coming to practice. I wasn't even sure he was going to show up. He had made promises before and then gotten called away to work. This time he had said he was coming to practice, which was at two-thirty, in the middle of his day.

He was there. He sat in the stands and watched us go through our drills and a minigame. I was so nervous, I couldn't do anything right. I couldn't catch the ball at all, and the one shot I took was an air ball from just behind the foul line. We finished our regular practice, and Mr. Evans motioned for my father to come down to the court.

"Your dad's a giant!" Kwame whispered as Dad came onto the court.

"That's how big Chris is going to be," Nicky G said.

I couldn't imagine ever being as tall as my father.

"I was watching the teams play the other day." Dad had both hands jammed into his pockets. "And I saw that neither of them were running baseline plays and almost all the shots were aimed for the rims. Shots off the backboards are going to go in a lot more than rim shots if you're shooting from the floor."

Dad picked up a basketball and threw it casually against the backboard. It rolled around the rim and fell through. He did it again. And again. He didn't miss once.

"I happen to know that you played pro ball," Mr. Evans said, "and you're good. But I think shooting from a wheelchair is a bit harder."

"You have another chair?" Dad asked.

Mr. Evans pointed to his regular chair sitting by the watercooler. Dad took four long steps over to it, sat down, and wheeled himself back onto the floor. He put his hands up and looked at me. I realized I was holding a ball and tossed it to him. He tried to turn his chair back toward the basket, and it spun all the way around. For a moment he looked absolutely lost, as if he didn't know what had happened to him. He seemed a little embarrassed as he glanced toward me.

"That happens sometimes," I said. "No problem."

He nodded, exhaled slowly, then turned and shot a long, lazy arc that hit the backboard and fell through.

"The backboard takes the energy out of the ball," he said. "So if it does hit the rim, it won't be so quick to bounce off. Madison made about twenty percent of its shots the other day. That doesn't win basketball games, no matter how good they look making them."

There are six baskets in our gym, and we spread out and practiced shooting against the backboards. At first I wasn't good at it. I was hitting the underside of the rim.

"That's because you're still thinking about the rim," Dad said when he came over to me. "Start thinking about a spot on the backboard. When you find your spot, really own it, you'll be knocking down your shots on a regular basis."

Nicky G got it first, and then Kwame, and then Bobby. I was too nervous to even hit the backboard half the time, but Dad didn't get mad or anything. He didn't even mumble. He just said it would come to me after a while.

Baseline plays were even harder. Dad wanted us to get guys wheeling for position under and slightly behind the basket.

"There are four feet of space behind the backboard," Dad said. "If you can use those four feet, you have an advantage."

We tried wheeling plays along the baseline but just kept getting in each other's way.

"That's the point," Dad said. "When you learn to move

without running into each other you're going to have a big advantage over a team that's trying to keep up with you."

Okay, so most of the guys are pretty good wheeling their chairs up and down the court. But our baseline plays looked more like a collision derby. Dad shook his head and Mr. Evans laughed.

We practiced all week. Dad came again and said we were improving.

"I thought you were terrible at first," he said, smiling. I didn't believe he actually smiled. "Now you're just pretty bad. But I think you can play with that Madison team."

Madison had agreed to come to our school to play, and when they arrived they were wearing jackets with their school colors and CLIPPERS across the back.

We started the game and Madison got the tip-off. The guy I was holding blocked me off so their guard, once he got past Nicky G, had a clear path to the basket. The first score against us came with only ten seconds off the clock.

I looked up in the stands to see where Mom was. I found her and saw Dad sitting next to her. I waved and she waved back, and Dad just sat there with his arms folded.

Madison stopped us cold on the next play, and when Bobby and Lou bumped their chairs at the top of the key, there was a man open. A quick pass inside and Madison was up by four.

We settled down a little, but nothing worked that well.

We made a lot of wild passes for turnovers, and once, when I was actually leading a fast break, I got called for traveling when the ball got ahead of me, and I touched the wheels twice before dribbling. The guys from Madison were having a good time, and we were feeling miserable. At halftime, we rolled into the locker room feeling dejected. When Dad showed up, I felt bad. He was used to winning, not losing.

"Our kids looked a little overmatched in the first half," Mr. Evans said.

"I think they played okay," Dad said, "just a little nervous. But look at the score. It's twenty-two to fourteen. With all their shooting, Madison is just eight points ahead. We can catch up."

I looked at Dad to see if he was kidding. He wasn't. He wasn't kidding, and he had said "we." I liked that.

We came out in the second half all fired up. We ran a few plays along the baseline, but it still seemed more like bumper cars than basketball with all the congestion. Madison took twenty-three shots in the second half and made eight of them plus three foul shots for a total score of forty-one points. We took seventeen shots and made eleven of them, all layups off the backboard, and two foul shots for a total of thirty-eight points. We had lost the game, but everyone felt great about how we had played. We lined up our chairs, gave Madison high fives before they left, and waited until we got to the locker room to give ourselves high fives.

Afterward, the team voted, and the Hartsdale Posse all agreed that we wanted to play in the league. Dad had shown us that we could play, and even though we had lost we knew we would be ready for the next season.

Dad only comes to practice once in a while, but he comes to the games when they're on the weekend. At practice he shows us fundamentals, stuff like how to line your wrist up for a shot, and how the ball should touch your hand when you're ready to shoot. That made me feel good even if he would never talk about the games when he wasn't in the gym. I didn't want to push it too much because I liked him coming to practice. I didn't want to push him, but Mom didn't mind at all.

"Jim, if you were in a wheelchair," she asked, "do you think you could play as well as Chris?"

Dad was on his laptop and looked over the screen at Mom, then looked over at me. Then he looked back down at the screen and grumbled something. I figured he was saying that there was no way he could play as well as me in a chair, but I didn't ask him to repeat it.

Acknowledgments

Two years ago, Ellen Oh was sitting at breakfast with Soman Chainani and Phoebe Yeh when she mentioned an idea she had for a WNDB anthology. Phoebe, as VP/Publisher at Crown Books for Young Readers, was immediately intrigued, and after Soman promised he'd write a story for it, the deal was struck and the rest was history.

WNDB is grateful to the dedicated and brilliant team at Crown/Random House, especially our wonderful editor, Phoebe Yeh, who brought this book to life, and our publisher, Barbara Marcus, who championed it from the very start. This anthology could not have happened without this amazing duo.

And our deepest gratitude to Barry Goldblatt, our extraordinary agent who takes such great care of us. WNDB couldn't have a better advocate.

And finally . . . We Need Diverse Books wouldn't exist without the incredible passion, energy, and hard work of our all-volunteer members. We are grateful to each author who contributed a story to this anthology, and to the special committee of WNDB members who read hundreds of entries to our short-story contest and selected a winner unanimously. Thank you, Elsie Chapman, Karen Sandler, Danette Vigilante, and Nicola Yoon.

About the Authors

Kwame Alexander's middle-grade debut, *The Crossover,* which the *New York Times* called "a beautifully measured novel," was a Newbery Medal winner, Coretta Scott King Honor, and *Publishers Weekly* Best Book of the Year. Alexander has written twenty-one books, including *He Said, She Said,* a Junior Library Guild selection; *Surf's Up;* and the award-winning children's book *Acoustic Rooster and His Barnyard Band.* His most recent middle-grade novel, *Booked,* is a *New York Times* bestseller. Kwame lives in Northern Virginia. Learn more about his work online at kwamealexander.com.

Kelly J. Baptist won the Ezra Jack Keats/Kerlan Memorial Fellowship for her YA novel-in-progress, *Young.* While visiting the Kerlan Collection, Kelly had the privilege of studying the dialogue techniques of the great Walter Dean Myers. Fast-forward a few years, and Kelly was fortunate enough to meet Myers at a literary event in Florida. A native of southwest Michigan, Kelly enjoys life with her husband

and five children, who give her plenty of inspiration for writing. Though her busy family life often results in having to type with one hand, Kelly is committed to using the written word to inspire and transform lives. Find her online at kellyiswrite.com.

Soman Chainani is an award-winning filmmaker and the *New York Times* bestselling author of the School for Good and Evil series, which has been translated into more than twenty-five languages. His film work has screened at hundreds of festivals worldwide, and *The School for Good and Evil* will soon be a major motion picture from Universal Studios, with Soman writing the screenplay. He grew up idolizing both Walt Disney and Madonna and is determined to find a career that allows him to be a little bit of both. His story "Flying Lessons" is based on the trips he took with his own glamorous, madcap Nani, who taught him that the greatest joys of the world are in its differences. Soman lives in New York City. Visit him online at somanchainani.net.

Matt de la Peña is the author of many critically acclaimed young adult novels, among them *The Living,* a Pura Belpré Honor Book; *Ball Don't Lie; Mexican White Boy; We Were Here;* and *I Will Save You.* He is also the author of the award-winning picture books *A Nation's Hope: The Story of Boxing Legend Joe Louis* (illustrated by Kadir Nelson) and Newbery Medal winner *Last Stop on Market Street* (illustrated by Christian Robinson). Matt says: "Walter Dean Myers is one of my greatest literary heroes. He was a brave, authentic storyteller who paved the way for all of the exciting diverse voices we're seeing in print today." Matt lives in Brooklyn, New York. Reach him online at mattdelapena.com.

Tim Federle's debut novel, *Better Nate Than Ever*, was named a *New York Times* Notable Children's Book and a Best Book of the Year by Amazon, *Publishers Weekly*, and Slate.com, in addition to receiving a Stonewall Honor. *Five, Six, Seven, Nate!*—the sequel to *Better Nate Than Ever*—won the Lambda Literary Award, and together the Nate books were called "one of the best new middle-grade series" by *School Library Journal*. With Claudia Shear, Tim is also the co-librettist of the Broadway musical adaptation of *Tuck Everlasting*. He believes that all kinds of kids deserve all kinds of stories. A native of Pittsburgh, Tim divides his time between New York and the Internet. Connect with Tim there on Twitter and Instagram at @TimFederle or on his website timfederle.com.

Grace Lin's Newbery Honor book *Where the Mountain Meets the Moon* was chosen for *Today*'s Al Roker's Book Club for Kids and was a *New York Times* bestseller. She is the author and illustrator of more than a dozen picture books, including *The Ugly Vegetables* and *Dim Sum for Everyone!* Her first early reader, *Ling & Ting,* was awarded a Theodor Seuss Geisel Honor. Most of Grace's books are about the Asian American experience, and she was recognized by the White House as a Champion of Change for AAPI Art and Storytelling in 2016. Her story "The Difficult Path" was partially inspired by Ching Shih, the legendary female pirate who ruled the sea during the Qing dynasty. Grace lives in Massachusetts and can be found online at gracelin.com.

Meg Medina is an award-winning Cuban American author who writes picture books, middle grade, and YA fiction. She won the Pura Belpré Award and the Cybils Award for Young Adult Fiction for her novel *Yaqui Delgado Wants to Kick Your Ass,* and a Pura Belpré Honor for her picture book *Mango, Abuela and Me.* Her most recent novel is *Burn Baby Burn.* Meg celebrates Latino families in her books by writing stories about how culture impacts the everyday drama of growing up. Meg lives with her family in Richmond, Virginia. Learn more about her online at megmedina.com.

Christopher Myers is a widely acclaimed author and illustrator who, in addition to illustrating his own titles, has collaborated with numerous authors, including E. E. Cummings, Zora Neale Hurston, and his father, Walter Dean

Myers. The two worked together on the Caldecott Honor winner *Harlem*, as well as the Coretta Scott King Honor winners *Black Cat* and *H.O.R.S.E.* Most recently he collaborated with dancer Misty Copeland on the picture book *Firebird*. Myers is a versatile artist, working with photos, gouache, woodcuts, collage, and other artistic media. His fine arts have been exhibited at MoMA PS1, Contrasts Gallery in Shanghai, the Prospect Biennial in New Orleans, and currently at the Cooper Gallery at Harvard. Myers also co-directed the documentary film *Am I Going Too Fast?* with Hank Willis Thomas, and recently designed a translation of the Egyptian Book of the Dead into a performance called *Go Forth*, directed by Kaneza Schaal. He has written several notable essays, among them "Young Dreamers," an eloquent reflection on Trayvon Martin and Ezra Jack Keats's *The Snowy Day*, as well as the much-discussed "The Apartheid of Children's Literature," published in the *New York Times* in 2014.

A prolific author of fiction, nonfiction, and poetry, **Walter Dean Myers** received every major award in the field of children's literature. He won two Newbery Honors, eleven Coretta Scott King Author Awards and Honors, three National Book Award finalists, and the first Michael L. Printz Award for Excellence in Young Adult Literature. He was the first recipient of the Coretta Scott King–Virginia

Hamilton Award for Lifetime Achievement. From 2012 to 2013, he served as the National Ambassador for Young People's Literature with the platform "Reading is not optional." *On a Clear Day, Juba!,* and *Monster: A Graphic Novel* were published posthumously. Myers's full list of works is available at walterdeanmyers.net.

Ellen Oh is cofounder and president of We Need Diverse Books (WNDB) and author of the YA fantasy trilogy the Prophecy series and the middle-grade novel *The Spirit Hunters,* to be published in fall 2017. She was named one of *Publishers Weekly*'s Notable People of 2014. Ellen met Walter Dean Myers and his son Christopher Myers at one of her first book festivals. Already nervous, her mouth dropped open when she saw the pair towering over the crowd. Chris took pity on an awestruck Ellen and introduced himself, and he and Walter couldn't have been nicer, taking her under their wing and treating her like an old friend. Oh resides in Bethesda, Maryland, with her husband and three children. Discover more at ellenoh.com.

Tim Tingle is a member of the Choctaw Nation of Oklahoma and the author of *Crossing Bok Chitto* and *How I Became a Ghost,* both winners of the American Indian Youth Literature Award. Raised in a highly athletic family, Tingle chose the basketball path. He kept journals of his off-court experiences in the late 1960s, as a starting point guard on an integrated college team, in a staunchly segregated community. When a friend gave him a copy of Walter Dean Myers's *Hoops* ten years later, Tim knew his own family's struggles, as Indians in modern America, could no longer be ignored. His latest YA novel, *House of Purple Cedar,* won the AIYL Award. Tim lives on the shores of Canyon Lake, Texas, and can be found online at timtingle.com.

Jacqueline Woodson is the sixth National Ambassador for Young People's Literature and is the author of the National Book Award winner *Brown Girl Dreaming,* four Newbery Honor books, three National Book Award finalists, a Coretta Scott King Award winner, and four Coretta Scott King Honor Books. She received the Margaret A. Edwards Award for her contributions to young adult literature and served as Young People's Poet Laureate. Her many award-winning novels include *Locomotion, After Tupac and D Foster, Beneath a Meth Moon, Each Kindness, Feathers,* and *Miracle's Boys.* She lives with her partner and two children in Brooklyn, New York. Find Jacqueline online at jacquelinewoodson.com.

About We Need Diverse Books

"Reading is not optional." This was Walter Dean Myers's platform when he served as the National Ambassador for Young People's Literature from 2013 to 2014. He said, "You can't do well in life if you don't read well." But Myers also believed that young people needed to see themselves reflected in the pages of the books they read. The goal of reaching out to these children through his books would become his life's work.

In his *New York Times* op-ed piece in November 1986, "Children's Books; I Actually Thought We Would Revolutionize the Industry," he wrote, "If we continue to make black children nonpersons by excluding them from books and by degrading the black experience, and if we continue to neglect white children by not exposing them to any aspect of other racial and ethnic experiences in a meaningful way, we will have a next racial crisis." More than twenty-five years later, he was dismayed to learn that according to a survey by the Cooperative Children's Book Center (CCBC), only 7.5 percent of the 3,600 children's book titles published in 2012 were about people of color.

On March 15, 2014, a month before the official launch of the We Need Diverse Books campaign, Christopher Myers and Walter Dean Myers wrote op-ed pieces for the *New York Times*. In "The Apartheid of Children's Literature," Chris wrote, "[Today's kids] see books less as mirrors and more as maps. They are indeed searching for their place in the world, but they are also deciding where they want to go. They create, through the stories they're given, an atlas of their world, of their relationships to others, of their possible destinations. . . . It's necessary to provide for boys and girls . . . a more expansive landscape upon which to dream."

In Walter's article "Where Are the People of Color in Children's Books?" he ended his appeal for more diversity with the urgent statement, "There is work to be done." This became the impetus for the We Need Diverse Books campaign, a rallying cry that brought advocates together from across the country, and around the world. The #WeNeedDiverseBooks hashtag went viral on social media platforms as people shared how important diversity was to them.

The idea behind We Need Diverse Books is not a new one—diversity advocates have championed the need for diverse books in children's literature for decades, and although the conversation continues beyond our reach, We

Need Diverse Books is grateful to be a part of this important movement. We create diversity initiatives in children's literature, sponsor internships and writers' grants, and administer the Walter Award, given to the teen novel that most embodies diversity and the work of Walter Dean Myers. And now, with this anthology, WNDB is honored to have ten talented authors join in the collaboration. For it is through notable partnerships like these that ideas take flight.